JED COPE

The Pipe

Copyright © 2021 by Jed Cope

All rights reserved. No part of this publication may be reproduced, stored or transmitted in any form or by any means, electronic, mechanical, photocopying, recording, scanning, or otherwise without written permission from the publisher. It is illegal to copy this book, post it to a website, or distribute it by any other means without permission.

This novel is entirely a work of fiction. The names, characters and incidents portrayed in it are the work of the author's imagination. Any resemblance to actual persons, living or dead, events or localities is entirely coincidental.

Jed Cope asserts the moral right to be identified as the author of this work.

First edition

This book was professionally typeset on Reedsy. Find out more at reedsy.com

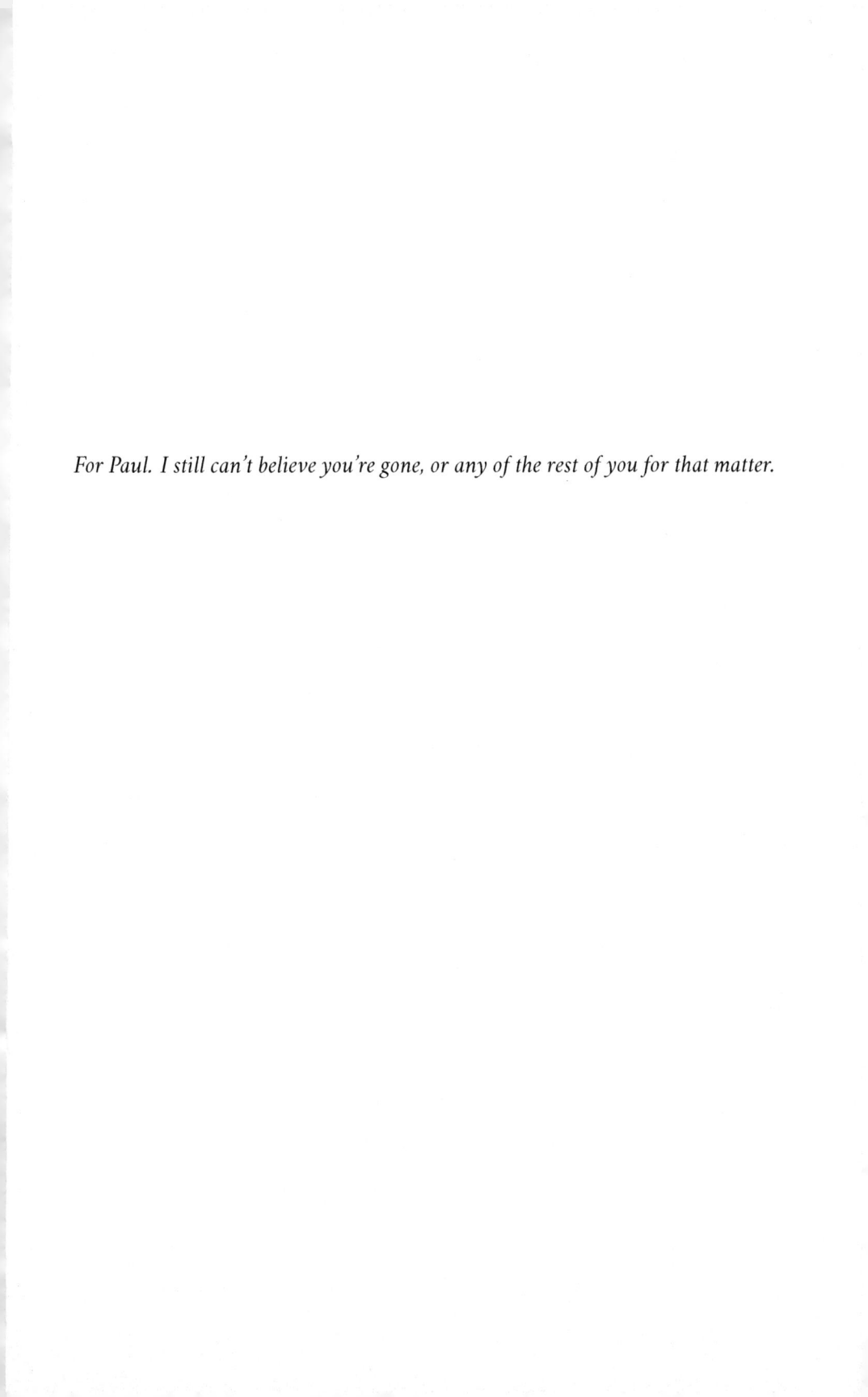

For Paul. I still can't believe you're gone, or any of the rest of you for that matter.

Foreword

I didn't write forewords in my first books. Then I decided that I should. I still approach the writing of this part with some degree of reluctance. That reluctance laces everything I do. I am a skilled procrastinator and I am prone to self-doubt. In this world we now live in, I suppose you would call me a troll, only I indulge only in self-trolling. Now I consider this more fully, I must get a kick out of this self-trolling, so there is an upside to it after all. A tarnished silver lining.

I wonder if the best things that we do are all like this? That we fear falling short and not being good enough, so we try to talk ourselves out of it…

"You don't have to do this."

"You should do a proper job with regular pay, you know."

"What if it's not good enough?"

That last is a constant. It stalks me day and night and I know what it really means.

"What if I am not good enough?"

I ride motorbikes and there is that same voice asking of me that same question. When I learnt to ride, I did so via a direct access course. We buddied up with an instructor, starting our riding on 125cc bikes and, half way through the third day of the course we switched to 500cc bikes. Big bikes. This was a course for the big bike licence. I remember the switch from not so little bike, not at the time anyway, to big bike. It was daunting, especially as the weight of the 500cc was significantly more than that of its smaller brother, and getting the thing off its centre stand required a knack that I did not have, having never rolled a bike off the stand before. I still have this fear of getting it all wrong when it comes to 'bike stands. My recurrent nightmare is dropping my bike outside a bike café and watching as it goes over in slow motion and takes the bike next it over, and the next, and the next…

I avoided bike cafés for several years after passing my test. Even though my love of bacon and the greasy spoon is infamous.

Some of the credit for my having passed my test and also for my approach to riding, must go to my buddy during that course. You see, on the first full day of riding the bigger bikes, we had turned up early on a cool summer's morning and we were walking towards the bikes when he cleared his throat and spoke up.

"I really thought I'd nailed this yesterday. Now I'm walking up to these buggers and I have to admit it. I'm bloody bricking it!"

The lad took the words right out of my mouth, and suddenly I didn't feel half as bad as I had. It was a relief to know it wasn't just me, and how often are we the chief architects of our own fear and our own demise. It is only in moments like this that we find that it is us who is building things up out of all proportion, but we're not alone in doing this.

More was to come though, because our instructor then answered him.

"Me too," he said quite simply.

This was a bit of a show stopper if I'm honest. You have to question the mentality of someone who is bricking it before climbing onto a piece of machinery, more so when he is responsible for not one, but two novices. If *he* was bricking it, then what hope did we have?

He must've known that his words would have an impact. He had our full attention now.

"Lads," he said, the three of us had now stopped in front of these scary, big motorbikes, "the day you stop being scared of these things, is the day that you fail to respect what they are and what it is that you are doing. On that day, or a day soon after that, you'll get yourself killed or something worse than killed."

Those words have lived with me ever since.

After passing my test, I went out and bought the same bike I passed on. A Honda CB500. This is classed as a big bike, but it was not big enough for me. So I bought another bike, a 600cc Bandit this time. I quickly outgrew that bike and wanted bigger, so I got myself a VFR750. Like many bikers, if not all of them, I have bikes that I wish I had never sold. That VFR was one of them. I traded up for a Fireblade at this point though, so it wasn't like I was slumming it.

I have to explain something. Bigger when it comes to motorbikes is relative. I don't think any of those bikes was significantly taller. The obvious size increase was the capacity of the engine. At that point though, I wanted to go faster. Faster on a motorbike is really about cornering, so the bike has to handle and it needs to be light and agile. It has to balance the extra weight that a larger engine brings with it against its ability to use that extra power.

I was learning along the way though. As you do as you embark upon a new venture. I kinda knew that bigger capacity engines didn't necessarily equate to more speed. And in my quest to ride different bikes and experience new things I bought bigger bikes. The Ducati Diavel may have been the biggest looking bike I have owned. It's a beast and by rights, it should be a bit of a pig to ride, but nothing could be further from the truth. Yes, it was a different proposition to a sportsbike, and that's why I wanted it, but it handled far better than it had any right to. I loved it.

It also scared me.

All of my bikes have scared me. And I've loved them all.

It's pretty much a ritual now, as I stand by my bike and get ready to ride it. I have to remember to calm the feck down as I put my gloves on. To reign it all back in and let that fear settle into something more useful. Then the adrenaline kicks in and off I go, my senses heightened in a way that you don't get in pretty much any other aspect of your life. Unless you do something insane, such as throw yourself out of a perfectly good airplane and rely on your bedsheet to slow your fall sufficiently so you don't die.

Head encased in a helmet and sitting with a container of petrol between your legs as explosions occur a little beneath that, and often sitting on top of a battery, which, should a small component called a regulator-rectifier fail, can boil the acid in said battery… that's happened on a hot summer's day. I thought it was the sun that was warming my most delicate of parts. It wasn't, and I was a very lucky boy that day! Hanging onto the grips and shifting your body to guide the bike while you use hands and feet to tinker with the engine and brakes so you can use the right amount of momentum to get you to where you need to go. Constantly assessing the road ahead of you. The road behind you. The roads to the side of you and looking out for that cager (car drivers, safely ensconced within their cars without a care for anyone's safety because *hey, I'm alright Jack*) who is intent on ending you in the very next second. Which is each and every one of them. Even the ones who make eye contact and acknowledge you might do something monumentally stupid directly after that. Moving from side to side as you approach a t-junction so that you stand a chance to be seen, because after several nonsensical near misses, you read about a phenomenon called motion camouflage, which means an object moving in a straight line towards someone, such as a dragonfly, can appear invisible. So lateral motion may help reduce this effect. *If* someone is bothering to look for you in the first place…

There's a famous cartoon biker, Ogri. Often a cager will attempt to kill him, and in their defence they will say they didn't see him, to which he will say, "you didn't look." Which is not him being pedantic. If you ever ride, you'll encounter of a sea of cagers who really don't bother looking. More so, now that smart phones are a window to our worlds and cars themselves have got in on the act, offering multi-media large screens that have to be more distracting than the speedo, rev counter, temperature and fuel gauges of old.

All of that is going on and more, and yet you see more of the world than you ever do in a car. I've noticed details out across the fields that I haven't seen when driving a convertible. Yes, I know I shouldn't be looking out across fields as I'm navigating my way through an army of homicidal cagers. The thing is that I'm not.

And there is no room for your mind to wander, so all of the ridiculous bullshit we all have a habit of getting caught up in is pushed away into the dark corners where it belongs and instead thoughts pop into your head. Good thoughts. Things that count. Because you're indulging in something that really counts.

People will regularly ask, "why do you ride? It's dangerous isn't it?"

The obvious reply to that is, "I ride because it's dangerous." This elicits frowns. I'm sorry, but if you know, you know. And if you don't? Either work on your empathy and try and meet people half way sometimes, or better still, learn to ride. The world would be a better place if everyone rode. The roads would be safer for starters!

Why have I written about my love of motorbikes? Well, I'm writing this foreword instead of doing the final edit. This is my writing ritual. I have to build up to the edit and the subsequent birth of my book into the world. Gird my loins and get into the necessary mindset. Then I crack on and just do it.

The thing with returning to a drafted book is I don't know what I'll find. It's been a while and I have high hopes for you my book. I want you to stand on your own two feet and do well out there. This is a very big moment.

Do you know what though, I think I'll sort the book cover first. I always have at least a good draft book cover. That gives me time to mull it and tweak it here and there. Besides, editing doesn't feel like writing. So I've taken to fitting the edits in around new writing. I write first drafts in the morning and then make time later for editing a book I previously drafted. I keep thinking that I should devote entire chunks of time to editing, but I fear should I stop writing...

...well, I may never start again.

The same as should I ever stop riding. Should I listen to that little voice that points out that I've not ridden that much over winter and so maybe it's time to hang my riding boots up, or least take a break from it? Well, I think that should I sell my bike, then that's my riding days over.

As we're talking about fear and my fear in particular, dear reader, I should address the elephant in the room. The Pipe is different to my previous books, isn't it?

I have pondered this. Have I tried to hedge my bets? Maybe in part. Just maybe.

The nub of it is, I read widely, so I struggle a bit with the restrictions of genre. I don't really get it. I didn't get people telling me that they can't read Sci Fi as though it were the peanut of books. What's the worst that can happen if you discover that the romantic, office drama you were reading turns out to be in the future. And in space? I'd be blown away if these were unexpected twists part way through a book I was reading.

Now horror? I get horror. I understand that some people will avoid gazing into the dark because the dark has a habit of staring right back at you and worse still, into you. We all want to be scared, but we all also have lines that we really don't want to cross. Like that line between light to dark…

…well, maybe some of us will venture into the dark a little way, just as long as we know the light is right there behind us. Others still will want to experience that disorienting feeling and the loss of self in the true pitch black. To fully understand what it is like to raise their hand and not to be able to see it. Not the movement, not a reflection of any light whatsoever. Maybe they do it to test themselves. Or they do it because they're with their friends and once one of them steps into the dark? Well, they all have to don't they?

Enjoy this book, dear reader, but make sure you keep a light on and you've checked the door is locked. Some things have a habit of creeping into the spaces that the darkness possesses, it's an invitation for them…

Now, if you'll excuse me, I'm going to grab my helmet and take my 'bike out. I can't talk about riding and not actually ride can I?! I mean, that's like talking about the amazing taste sensations of curry and then not ordering a curry that very evening…

Jed Cope
June 2021

1

It is that time of year when The Sun climbs languorously to the top of the sky and hangs around for an age as though she's suspended in a hammock, enjoying an ice cold drink and kicking the shit. She's in no rush. She looks down upon the town and enjoys the view. She watches the world go by and her enjoyment has a scurrilous edge. Many adults lose their way as the years pass, and this means that they lose their sense of fun too. They seem to think that they are the world and all that matters. If she were so minded, The Sun would be angered by such petty mindedness, but this is a long summer and she intends for it to be one that will be indelibly marked in the collective memory of these people. Years from now, even the man currently mopping his brow with his hanky and moaning about how damnably hot it is as though this is a terrible thing, even he will look back upon these days as halcyon.

The Sun sees all. The closed minds and perceptions of the people below are alien to her. She is timeless and limitless. So, even as she notes the moaning man and the chorus of others who have prayed to her every day to come and light up their days and banish the dread and gloom of the winter months, she sees also sights that fill her with wonder and happiness. These strange and contradictory creatures can do that. For a time. There are moments that define them and make them worthwhile. The Sun will miss them when they are gone. They have been a wonderful episode in The Sun's existence. Sadly it will be a short one. Their miracle will end at their own hands. They can see it as well as she can, but still they head to a conclusion which will see this planet that they consider to be theirs falter and perhaps die. The Sun hopes it will survive, but she doubts she will be as entertained by whatever life thrives and evolves after these creatures have passed.

* * *

There was a loud snap, a good deal of rustling and then a crash which was the accompanying soundtrack to the small boy's arrival.

"Archie!" cried another small child who had made her way to this forest clearing in a slower, quieter and more considered manner. The respective personalities of the two children could be seen reflected in the way they had made their way here to this clearing.

"Charlie!" cried Archie and theatrically stumbled the last few steps to his friend and then collapsed into her arms in mock exhaustion.

There was a moment there when Charlie held Archie and that would have been an end to it, but Archie was the bigger of the two children and he presented a dead weight to his friend. Charlie groaned with the effort of lifting him and preventing calamity, but it was too much for her and she collapsed like a sack of spuds. The larger sack of spuds collapsed heavily on top of her, winding her. There was laughter, but the laughter was one sided.

There was more to be learned from the respective personalities of the children from this moment.

Once he was done with laughing, Archie clambered up. He did not offer Charlie his hand. We're coming to expect that outcome already. Archie will not grow out of these behaviours. As this is the case, we hope that Charlie won't lose any of her compassion, loyalty and empathy. We could live with that deal. Archie would do well to stick with Charlie, she's a good friend and he is better for being around her. This should work both ways, and it does in a fashion. That's friendship for you.

"Where's Kabir?" asked Charlie as she dusted herself off. She rubbed at a grass stain, trying to remove the worst of it, knowing that her mum was going to have words with her and probably note the accompanying bruises that she regularly received courtesy of her best friend, "He's too rough with you! I bet he doesn't have bruises!" She had never quite forgiven Archie for chipping Charlie's front tooth. That was nearly five years ago. They're ten now. For a ten year old, that was a lifetime ago.

Still, despite how much she pissed and moaned about the brute who is Archie, her mum was always nice to him when he came over to their house, sweet even. Charlie may only be ten, but she can see that Archie has a certain something. He sparkles and he dazzles. In those moments, he is not her friend Archie, he is something else. Charlie is not sure whether she likes the dazzling Archie. That Archie is a bit too shiny and, well, he isn't Archie anymore. Not really. She cannot disagree that he is entertaining and has a certain special quality. But she knows that he gets away with things when he switches to this Archie. He gets his own way and controls people and this leaves Charlie uncomfortable. She wonders if he uses Special Archie on her, and if he ever did, would she know?

Archie has opened her eyes to how blind people, herself included, can be.

Archie shrugged as Charlie asked where Kabir was. He didn't know where Kabir was. Nor did he care. He'd made his way here under his own steam and so had Charlie, so he assumed that Kabir would too. That's just how it was.

As if summoned by her question, there was another rush of rustling as something crashed through the undergrowth of the forest. It was nearing the clearing and drawing the attention of both children. Their curious faces transformed into beaming smiles as their friend burst forth and threw himself to the ground now he had arrived at the end of a long, frantic and arduous journey.

He lay face down and panting long enough for Charlie and Archie to assemble around him. Once he sensed their presence, either side of him, he rolled over and grinned at his friends.

Charlie reached a hand down to help Kabir up. Archie mirrored the gesture so they both pulled him to his feet.

"Did you bring it?" asked Archie with an urgency in his voice.

Kabir had still to get his breath back, he breathed a yes through his laboured breathing and nodded vigorously to supplement his struggling voice.

"Let's see!" said Archie excitedly, bounding around him like a possessed kangaroo.

Kabir held a finger up and turned, keeping his back and the rucksack on it away from Archie. Archie grabbed at it anyway, he could not contain himself. He wanted to see it. He *would* see it. The boys tussled and Charlie steppe back, not wanting to get caught with a flying limb. She almost misjudged her timing; a satellite hand orbiting the melee, pecked her cheek with puckered lips of air as it sped by. She stepped further back, working out how to intervene. She did not want either of her friends to go too far. More importantly, she didn't want the contents of the rucksack to be broken. That would ruin the mission.

Archie got a purchase on the rucksack and now had the advantage, it was all but over. He held on and Kabir, with his back to his foe could only jerk and wriggle. Archie now unzipped the main part of the bag and reached in. Stealing the object and with it, Kabir's moment. Archie withdrew his hand and raised the object aloft like King Arthur himself. He did not have to bellow 'Behold!' his exultant face and triumphant posture said it all.

They had their torch. It was big and it was metallic. The metal casing shone in the sunlight and almost blinded Charlie. She looked away from the shining surface, but retained the image of Archie. She also noted the look Kabir gave Archie. A look that was gone in an instant, but was enough to convey Kabir's unhappiness, his displeasure at what his friend had done. He rallied swiftly to the raised talisman remembering why the three had come here this day. It was he who initiated the cheer and Charlie and Archie joined with him. They were the stuff of legends, and what they were to do this very day would go down in history.

And this would be a legendary summer. The Sun had made sure of it, and she was not finished yet. She would keep at this Summer for three more months and even then she would linger a while longer. By the time she was done, the earth beneath the children's feet in this clearing would be parched and cracked. A few yellowed patches of grass clinging on in desperate hope of rain. Rain that was sometimes promised and occasionally

1

made an appearance, but only long enough to remind everyone of what they were missing out on. When The Sun was in her sky and felt like sticking around, the rain was deposed and it would have to damn well wait until The Sun was good and ready to accede the sky to the gloomy interloper.

Archie lowered the torch and looked from Charlie to Kabir. Kabir's hopes of having the torch back were dashed in that moment. Archie had the torch, it was his Excalibur and it was he who would lead his knights to the field of battle.

Nothing was said. He merely nodded at each of his friends and they nodded solemnly back.

The Sun watched dispassionately, knowing what awaited them and that were they to know what she already knew, two of them would abandon this venture of theirs in a heartbeat. The other would not. The other had it within them to bring those two with him, even as they harboured the gravest of misgivings. This was dangerous, and he was dangerous. Perhaps one of the two would prevail. Not with reason alone, but with a force of will that was equal to her friend's. This would leave the balance of power with the third friend. The Sun knew that once people gathered and combined to be a group or crowd, there was no knowing which way they would turn, only that the odds were usually on a course of action that none of the individuals in the group would have chosen and a path that invariably ended up in a bad place.

The Sun saw them and loved them unconditionally. It was all she knew and she celebrated the miracle of their existence for them as they were too caught up in living to appreciate how wonderful they were.

The three children formed a line and marched out of the safety of the clearing and on to their objective. Soon enough, the forest closed in around them and on them. It grew denser and denser. This was a path less travelled and barely a path in places. This was a track used by small animals who would not be bothered by the numerous branches which slapped and grabbed at the three children. Archie's leadership in this theatre was disastrous, he was completely unaware of the havoc he wreaked behind him and it took a while for Kabir to adjust his own strategy and his distance from the vanguard so that the branches sprang back into place directly after Archie's passage and ceased their attack on him.

There was something dark and grim about this part of the woods. The green tinged darkness itself was oppressive, and despite the wealth of vegetation, there seemed to be fewer creatures here. It was as though they sensed that there was something wrong here and they avoided it. The oppression of this place was coupled with a fading of sound as well as light. The bird song came from far away. Further away than the children had walked. They had entered an alien place and the invisible walls of this land muted the outside world.

Charlie felt it the most and she could see from the change in Kabir's movements that he must be feeling it too. He became more considered and cautious as they went deeper into that forest. Archie however, soldiered on. He seemed unaffected by his surroundings. He was Archie and the world had to take note of him! Kabir and Charlie had to up their pace as a gap opened up between them and Archie. They didn't want to lose him. The thought of that scared Charlie. The only reason they were here was Archie. He was the brave one and he had instilled courage within Charlie, the courage she needed to be here right now.

Charlie was no scaredy cat and she doubted that Kabir was either. She slept with all the lights out and has done so for more than two years. She loved to adventure and discover and the thought of this endeavour had filled her with delight. She had looked forward to it and day dreamed about it, switching themes as she imagined the trio as pirates one moment, soldiers the next and one imagining even had them as space men.

A child's imagination is a wonderous thing, it knows no bounds and can take them anywhere. Right now, Charlie's imagination was taking her to places she really didn't want to be. And she really didn't want to be here right now. There was barely any sound, so she could hear her own breathing, feel the very beginnings of panic and terror. She wondered how strong she could be and how close she were to tears. She could feel them there, waiting. They were making themselves known to her which was a very bad sign. She worried that one of her friends would see them and make fun of her for being

1

scared.

Kabir kept looking back at her. The initial relief of seeing the obvious fear on his face quickly faded to be replaced with further doubt that led to her own fear building. It wasn't just her then. Kabir was making the basis for her own fear more real and she could feel it's solidity as they moved further into this part of the woods. There was something off about this place. They should not be here. This was a place for dark things and if you entered then you better be dark, or you better be darn sure you could fend off the dark things and make your way back into the light.

They had been here once before. It had been spooky then too. But that was the first time, and plenty of places held some dark in the mystery of a first encounter. Familiarity dispelled that dark. Not this time it didn't. This time it was worse. It was worse for having visited here that time before. They should have known after that first time that they were not welcome here.

The first time had been a warning. They had been warned.

Once was a mistake and you had better learn from it. The second time was a choice and now they would face the consequences. They were going to pay.

Charlie could feel eyes on her. She looked around but could see nothing but the forest. She felt like the forest itself was looking at her, she could feel that now. It was cold. Colder than it had any right to be in this summer heat, and the light was that of a different time and place. Something other than the forest was watching them as well. Something that lurked and watched and then picked it's time to emerge from the trees to make itself known once and once only. It only ever showed itself the once. Once was enough.

Charlie grabbed at Kabir's arm. She hadn't even known she was going to do it. Kabir stiffened and looked back at her. She looked at him pleadingly. They should stop. They should go back. There was a grim determination on Kabir's face. She could see that he was not for turning. Knew that he was scared, but he had now come too far, he'd passed the tipping point and was following Archie blindly. Kabir would follow Archie, come what may.

Charlie nodded. She didn't even consider turning back now. She couldn't. These were her friends. She couldn't leave them. Her loyalty bound her to them right now and whatever happened, she would be there with them.

The forest didn't exactly open up. This was not a clearing. It did offer up a mystery though. A dark and foreboding mystery. How The Pipe had come to be here was as much a mystery as what was in The Pipe. That it had been here for a long time was clear. It was as much a part of this place as the trees. And yet it was not of this place, or rather it should not have been a part of a forest. The Pipe made this place different and strange and that was what had drawn the children here the first time. They had run from that place only slowing once they had made the safety of their own, familiar clearing. Ignorant of the cuts and grazes their careening return had inflicted upon them and in that moment of relief, having survived that dark adventure they had made a mad promise, born of the excitement of their successful escape from that brooding and fearsome place.

They were going back.

Only this time, they were coming back with a torch and they were going to go into that tunnel, into The Pipe, and find out where it led.

That was their promise and that was their plan. Light up The Pipe with a big torch that would give them plenty of light because it was a big tunnel with plenty of dark. Once they had the torch though, things would be different. They would dispel the darkness and things wouldn't be so bad after all. Then they would march right into The Pipe with their torch lighting the way and they would uncover its secrets.

They would discover The Pipe's treasure and claim it for their own.

Fame and fortune beckoned.

Now they were here, looking into the darkness within The Pipe. Looking at the disk of black that afforded not even a glimpse of what lay and lurked within. They had the means to illuminate that darkness and venture forth. To go into The Pipe and discover its mysteries.

They stood in a semi-circle around the entrance to The Pipe. Archie had not stolen the moment and bowled in without pause. This was a ledge and had to be considered. The entire forest seemed to gather around this spot. It was an epicentre. A focal point.

But for what?

1

"Shall we?" Archie's voice was quiet and somehow diminished.

Hearing it made Charlie feel small and helpless. The monsters of her early childhood had never left her. She knew that now. All she'd done was learn that the monsters were not under her bed, or hiding in her wardrobe. That they dwelt elsewhere. But now she knew that they existed, that they were very real and that they waited, and every now and then they did take a child. And if ever she was in the presence of a monster it was here and now. Only… it felt like the monster wasn't in The Pipe right now. The Pipe may well be its lair, but it was out there in the forest and it was watching them intently as they considered trespassing, as they considered entering its inner sanctum.

There was only one entrance and so there was only one exit. If the monster was so minded, it could easily trap them once they were inside. They would have to go through the monster in order to escape.

Neither Kabir or Charlie responded to Archie's question. They were almost hypnotised, paralysed by the impenetrable darkness awaiting them. The silence drew out.

CLICK!

There was a sudden, sharp report somewhere off behind them, back the way they had come. Charlie swore she heard a slight whirring as the three friends looked around them.

"What was that?" asked Kabir. He was scared, almost to the point of losing it.

Archie smiled his Dazzling Archie smile and patted Kabir's upper arm, "Come on," he turned then, stepping into the dark void. Showboating, choosing not to switch the torch on until they were all enclosed in the darkness of The Pipe.

2

The children disappeared into The Pipe.

The Pipe swallowed them whole.

His Pipe. The Pipe was his, all of it was his. They were trespassing! The dirty little fuckers were in *his* place! He rocked to and fro, unable to contain himself, but not knowing what to do. Beside himself with inexplicable rage and an emptiness that threatened to consume him. He needed The Bad Man right now, but The Bad Man would not come.

He would have to wait. The Bad Man always came. And these days he came along regularly. The boy and The Bad Man had an *understanding*.

The boy sat and he watched and he waited. Barely noticing his mouth moving and the words quietly spilling out…

Row row row your boat
Gently down the stream
If you see a crocodile don't forget to
Row row row
Row row row
Row row row

His voice growing coarser, growling the word *row* again and again and again. Blood combined with the spital that flecked his lips.

Row row row
Row row row
Row row row

2

***

The dark swallowed them up and enveloped them.

Any and every residue of the outside winked out. No gradual fading. It was gone. No sight. No sound. There was The Pipe and that was all there was. The Pipe was everything and it was nothing.

Charlie was cocooned in a dark that she had never before encountered. It was intense. She could feel it. It clothed her. It was total.

She knew she was looking in Archie's direction or at least where she had last seen him, but her eyes saw nothing. They were open, but she was blind. What made it all the worse was she could not hear him. She could not hear Kabir. It were as though her senses had been switched off and in this moment, she was totally alone and completely lost.

Charlie raised a hand in front of her face. It was not there. It did not exist.

She, Charlie, no longer existed.

She was scared, but strangely calm right now. As though she were floating in the liquid darkness. That could not be right, could it? But then this place was not right. There was something very wrong about this place and they had been drawn into it. Charlie had gone against all of her instincts, instincts that had screamed *no* to her. Told her not to do this thing. Told her to run from this place and to never, ever come back.

The first time hadn't been like this. The first time there had only been mystery and the desire to adventure. To come back with a torch and explore. She'd thought of nothing else and neither had Archie or Kabir. They had talked excitedly about their return and what they might find in The Pipe. There was a secret within The Pipe, they knew it the first time they'd seen it. Treasure. They'd convinced each other it was treasure. There had to be something concealed in The Pipe and it was down to the three of them to discover it.

They'd already agreed to split the spoils equally three ways and talked about how their lives would change. How their new found riches would allow them to fulfil their wildest dreams. And they would share that adventure together too. They would buy three neighbouring mansions and build tunnels and underground spaces so they could move freely between each of their homes. They would have a shared lair where they would plan their escapades and then ride out together on missions of vital importance to the nation. They were heroes in the making. With the vast wealth that awaited them, the world would know them and love them for all their heroic deeds. Charlie had added acts of kindness and great generosity and the two boys had grudgingly mumbled that they supposed they could do a bit of that too. That bit didn't sound as exciting or heroic. Charlie had wanted to explain that true heroes had hearts of gold and that their kindness and mercy were the most important bit, but the moment was lost in an impromptu testosterone fuelled duel between Archie and Kabir as they demonstrated their super hero powers.

The lure of this place had been powerful, it had even visited Charlie in her dreams and without asking the other two, she knew it was the same for them. The Pipe had drawn them here. It had wanted them to come. There was something seductive and compelling about the place they had dreamed about, both in their sleep and during their days.

This was not the same place they had visited on that first occasion. This place was cold and unwelcoming. It was ancient and deadly. There was a terrible hunger about it.

All that Charlie wanted now was for Archie to switch that torch on and for them to get out of this place. To get this over and done with as quickly as possible. This was no longer fun. Where was the light? They'd only taken a few steps inwards and the light had gone. That wasn't even possible! Was it?

Charlie wanted to speak. She wanted to tell Archie to turn the torch on, but her voice would not come. There was something in here with them and if she made a sound it would find her. She bit her lower lip, stifling a sob.

Then there was light. Sudden, glorious transformative light. Light that revealed Archie and Kabir and a damp, brickwork tunnel. No creature of the darkness looming over them about to devour one of their number. The interior of The Pipe, now illuminated seemed smaller and far less exotic. Ordinary even. Charlie's breathing returned to normal and she admonished her imagination, told it off for taking her some place else and scaring the living hell out of her.

"Cool!" said Kabir quietly.

Cool? thought Charlie? Really!?

"I've never been anywhere that dark!" continued Kabir, as if responding to Charlie's unspoken words, "I couldn't even see my hand in front of my face!"

"And it felt much bigger in the dark didn't it?" grinned Archie, "I couldn't find the walls with my hands and I was stumbling around like a little old lady!"

Charlie forced a smile for her friends. Did they not feel it? There was something really bad here. The silence gave her the creeps. A silence only punctuated by an invisible drop of water, falling and finding a puddle that she could not see. Unbidden, she imagined that the liquid that was drip, drip dripping was blood. A puddle of blood. She shuddered. She looked at her friends wondering what they were thinking and feeling, not coming away with much of anything other than an excited determination to forge on ahead.

Archie waved the torch around in the direction her was intending to take them, deeper into The Pipe.

"What's that!?" he said theatrically.

Charlie wanted to tell him to quit it. It wasn't funny.

"What?" Kabir's voice an equal measure of wonder and fear.

That was Archie's cue to stride forward and for the other two to move quickly with him for fear of being left behind by the circle of light.

They should have brought a torch each, thought Charlie. She was at the back and struggling to keep up with everything. She was walking in the memory of the light, focusing on the light ahead and following the other two. Most of what she could see was their backs and they obscured most of the lit area.

Surely the torch should be illuminating more than the small circle that it was? The light beyond that circle was total and seemed to be pushing forth against the light, eager to extinguish it. The dark was a living thing. Charlie had never known anything like it

Archie was moving quickly, eager to find whatever was at the end of the tunnel. The secrets of The Pipe and the promise of treasure was all that mattered to him and the sooner they found it, the sooner they would fulfil all of their day dreams and more.

Charlie caught fleeting images of things carved in the brickwork. At first, it was an occasional etching. The markings seemed to be of figures. Of people and animals. As they went deeper into The Pipe, the frequency of the images intensified until there were as many images as there were untouched areas of brickwork.

Then the brickwork changed. The bricks giving way to sandstone. Old, large blocks of sandstone worn away in places. Then the blocks themselves seemed to fade until there were no seams, they were now in a long, cavernous tunnel. A cave. The images were continuing to grow in frequency, building and building, until…

"Wow!" gasped Archie.

Kabir crashed into his back, "Ouch, you idiot!" cried Archie. The torchlight wavered wildly as Archie stumbled.

Charlie's heart was in her mouth, she could see the torchlight lurching and she imagined the torch leaving Archie's hand and then, as it landed and broke into a hundred pieces, absolute darkness would encase them and take them. She didn't know what they would do if that happened. The thought of it terrified her. She was relieved to see the light stabilise and a sort of calm was restored, albeit her heart rate only stepped down one notch. She was not at all comfortable here. She'd be glad when they emerged back in the daylight and even then they would have to run the gauntlet of the foreboding forest. At least she was with her friends. She could not do this alone.

She chose to ignore the fact that she would not have done this and she would not be here, were she alone.

Charlie edged nearer to Kabir and Archie and peered past them to see what Archie had stopped in front of. She didn't think for a moment that it was treasure, but what she saw in front of Archie and Kabir could well be a prelude to treasure.

The images filled the rock face in a belt in front of and around the old rusted metal work of a gate and its frame. Charlie could see the images going on beyond this. This was the entrance proper. A huge and substantial iron structure embedded so far into the surrounding stone that it had grown to become a part of it. The gate itself was relatively small. It were as though it had been designed specifically to allow someone the size of a ten year old to pass through. An adult would have had to stoop low in order not to hit their head. All the same, the gate was thick and heavy, you could tell this just by looking at it.

Charlie looked at the hinges, they were encrusted in rust and it was doubtful that the gate had been opened in a long, long time. She found that she was relieved at the prospect of this being journey's end, courtesy of an impassable gate that had rusted shut forever. This structure had been built to keep people out. Or worse still, to keep something *in*. Charlie shuddered at the thought of this. Something ancient and terrible that lived in the bowels of the Earth. Kept at bay by a huge metal cage. That was what it reminded her of. A cage. Prison bars.

Someone had built this prison to keep a terrible evil out of the world.

Archie stepped forward and clutched at the gate itself. He pulled and pushed, his efforts becoming more urgent as nothing happened, not even a rattling of metal against metal. Although the thickness of this metal would give off a dull and sonorous clang were it to be hit.

"Der!" said Kabir to Archie's back and Charlie's heart sank as Kabir stole this moment in swift retribution for Archie's earlier scene stealing. Kabir stepped forth and pulled the large metal bolt he'd spotted and now the gate was unlocked.

The sound was all wrong, it was smooth and sure and reassuring. That just did not fit with the look of this gate.

It were as though something wanted Kabir to slip that bolt back and unlock the gate.

Archie looked back at Kabir and scowled at him, unhappy at having been upstaged. It was a fleeting moment as Archie was intent on taking back control, he had hold of the gate and it was he who pushed it open.

There was no way that the gate should have opened!

Charlie could see that the gate was rusted shut. There should have been no way that Archie could have opened it, not without a fight anyway. But there it was, opening easily with no semblance or pretence of opposition. No, it was welcoming them in. It wanted them to step through and continue into The Pipe. The rusty, unoiled hinges did not even whisper a protest as they opened.

Charlie wanted to question this. Question her friends. Ask them to *think about this.* It wasn't right! Could they at least pause their adventure and come back another day?

She knew that neither Archie or even Kabir would listen to her. Not right now. They would probably call her chicken and make fun of her and she couldn't do with that. She needed them. They needed each other, now more than ever.

Besides, the moment was fleeting and it was lost, they were already entering the inner sanctum. The place that had been closed and secured and now was wide open to them.

As Charlie stepped over the lower part of the iron work that the gate had been set into, her foot landed upon something solid and circular. Her foot did not gain purchase and she slipped. Somehow, she managed to find her footing and didn't cry out. The others carried on ahead of her.

She caught her breath and something made her crouch and feel for what it was that she had stood on. Her hand found cold, slightly rough metal. A large loop of it that was inside another, another identical loop which was inside another. A chain. A huge chain at the foot of a big, substantial set of bars and a gate. The gate had been bolted and chained shut. Charlie could see it in her mind's eye. Yet now the chain lay discarded at the foot of the metalwork barring the way. She shivered as she considered the possibilities. Treasure was not one of them.

The chain and lock had been removed. Who had done that? And why?

The torchlight was receding. She panicked and quickly she went after the other two and the comparative safety of the light, walking as quickly as she possibly could without breaking into a run. She did not want to fall. She imagined what it would be like to catch her foot and twist her ankle. To be left here whilst Kabir and Archie went for help. She thought she would go mad if she were left here alone. This was a place of madness and the intensity of that feeling was building within her. Threatening to undo her. She could feel the images on the walls around her. Somehow, even in this darkness, she knew they were everywhere. On the walls, the ceiling and even on the floor. She was walking on them. They seemed to be alive. Moving. Watching.

She caught up with her friends. Glad to be near them again. The Pipe could not go on much further could it? She wondered how much longer it felt to move along this dark and oppressive space than it would to cover the same ground in the open daylight. She knew that the depravation of her senses was making this space seem different. Confusing and disturbing her. A thought came from nowhere. They had been travelling downwards without realising it. That was a certainty. The Pipe went underground and it kept going down.

They were going deeper. Into the Earth.

Archie slowed.

"What is it?" asked Kabir, his voice containing a slight tremor.

Archie lifted a hand to silence him. He'd seen the gesture in a war film and thought it to be very cool. Had wanted to use it. To highlight not only how cool he was, but also to demonstrate his superiority and control. This seemed like the best time to use it and it felt good. Now he'd used it and enjoyed it's effect, he'd definitely use it some more.

The three stood there suspended in time. Then there was a strange sighing sound. A sound like a dragon's sleepy sigh, thought Charlie. They felt a gentle blast of warm fetid air on their faces. There was the hint of something truly awful in that breath. That hint lingered. It not only lingered, but it built and grew and dialled itself up until it filled The Pipe. A ripe stench of dead things.

"Eeewww! What was that!" Archie was almost giggling.

Charlie did not find it funny though. Far from it.

Kabir was gagging, "that was awful!"

Charlie vaguely recalled something about poison air in mines. Miners taking canaries down into the mines to detect the poison because it was odourless. Did the smell mean they were OK? She didn't feel at all OK. Her flesh was creeping and she felt violated and unclean.

The smell dispersed and dropped in intensity, but it remained in The Pipe. None of them questioned how until they smelt the stench, there had been no odour to The Pipe at all, and now they could smell something rank. Whatever lay ahead of them, Charlie doubted that it was gold, silver and gems.

Archie didn't confer with either of his friends, he did what he always did, making an executive decision to move on, knowing that where he went, others would follow.

When Charlie thought about that day, she thought that perhaps this was the final point of no return. That if she had said something, then maybe they could have turned around and left that place and everything would have been OK. Even better if Kabir had spoken up, because Charlie would have backed him all the way and surely with both of them set upon a retreat, Archie would have conceded. He could not have gone on without them. He might have tried, but he would have had to turn back, after all, they all needed that torch and it was Kabir's torch. They would have had to stick together.

But it was not to be. Archie was single minded. They had come this far, why in hell would they not see this through? As far as Archie was concerned, they had to continue onwards. So they did.

The Pipe seemed to gently snake now. There was something even more disconcerting with the way it moved. It was no longer a straight tunnel. This made it organic somehow, and it was no stretch of the imagination to see The Pipe as a giant and terrible living thing. The kinks in its sides moving and changing. They were going further into the belly of the beast and deeper down into the Earth.

The stench was building. Occasionally one of them would cough as the smell crawled into their mouths and clambered down into their throats. None of them said anything now. They shared a grim determination to see this thing through. They would see it through to the very end.

When Charlie thought back to that day, she would swear that The Pipe was playing tricks on them. That it was amplifying the intensity of the dark and everything that went with that dark so that they were even more disoriented. It was much more than that though, she tried not to think about how it seemed to know a part of them. That it was quietly whispering to each of them. It was playing with them and it was playing them.

The end came suddenly and horribly. They had all thought that their objective was still a fair distance off. They knew that. They could sense it. They could feel it. They had an unfounded confidence in the proceedings and that came crashing down around them as they turned the next corner expecting nothing other than more of the same and to continue onwards and downwards. If anything, they had a growing fear that The Pipe would never end. That they would keep on and on and on, going further and deeper into the stinking bowels of the Earth.

That isn't what happened though. None of them would ever fully recount what happened next. It was doubtful that any of them could have, even if they had tried. Each of them had a piece of it, the rest of it broiled and moved and slipped in and out of their consciousness. Lower down, deep inside of themselves they related to that moment in an instinctual and deeply emotional way.

They encountered evil in that next moment and some of it clung onto them. It stuck with them and would never let them go.

They would never be the same again.

Archie rounded the corner. They had a slow, but steady pace now. They stayed bunched up, but with enough room that none of them were touching. They were marching in time like good little soldiers one minute, but as the second hand touched the twelve to end that minute, it ushered in chaos.

The next bit was in extreme slow motion. Time was broken and twisted from then on. Some parts would speed past. Others would blink away so quickly as to be lost.

Charlie supposed that Archie lost his footing. That he had stepped upon something viscous and slippery and that was why the torch arced away and upwards affording a flash of something so terrible that even that fleeting glimpse was enough to unhinge all three of them, because as they saw it, something within them took control. They did not think, they just went. Charlie grabbed for Archie and pulled him up and away. Kabir was doing the same thing.

There was death here. Lots of it.

That was what was at the end of The Pipe.

Death and evil.

Oblivion.

They had been walking blindly into the jaws of death, but it was worse than that. This was not just an end. It was the worst of ends. It was pain and tortured fear and a slow, lingering death. It was looking into the eyes of your tormentor and in them seeing nothing but madness. Succumbing to the madness and eventually being consumed by it. Joining with the evil and wishing for the release of death even as your mind let go.

They ran.

They ran for their lives.

The torch swinging wildly. Making a macabre lightshow of The Pipe. Something was chasing them and the noises it was making were not of this world. The vision of what they had seen lingered. It would stay with them until the day they died.

Charlie, Kabir and Archie left something of themselves in The Pipe that day and that summer was the end of their childhood proper. They lost what remained of their innocence and grew up in the most terrible of ways.

3

Oft times, the return journey is shorter and easier than the outward journey, and there's some puzzlement as to why the first journey was so long and fraught. The opposite was true as three terrified children ran away from something so terrible they would never speak of it again. Not with each other, nor with anyone else. So terrible was that day that they would eventually drift away from each other so that they were no longer reminded of what they had seen, of what they had experienced together and what they had all been afforded a glimpse of.

Three friends who were so close that everyone assumed that they would have been friends for life. They should have been and as it turned out, they still were. Only they could not look at each other without seeing something dark and terrible too. Without reliving a moment of their time in The Pipe and eventually it was too much.

Each provided a mirror to the darkness within them and they could not bear to gaze upon that image.

The Pipe seemed to have grown as they had ventured into it. However hard they ran, however much they tried. The gate did not appear. It was a waking nightmare where the laws of physics were discarded by everything other than the dreamer. They were crying as they ran. They dare not slow and they dare not turn their heads. They went on regardless. They could not stop, they could not even look behind them, or all would be lost.

There was barely any relief as they saw the gate, they knew that this was only a marker point and the finish line was still a way off.

The Pipe had not finished with them yet.

Then they saw something that almost undid them. The gate was shut.

* * *

The Bad Man was coming now. The sun was waning and the boy knew that the Bad Man was on his way. He could feel him. The boy had a connection with the Bad Man. The Bad Man preferred the dark. This was a problem for the boy as he was not allowed out after dark, but he found ways to sneak out and get away unobserved so that he could see the Bad Man and do his bidding.

The Bad Man was angry. He was very angry. The boy figured that his anger was something to do with the three fuckers who had trespassed on their turf. They had no right to go into The Pipe! It was *his*. It was *theirs*.

The boy hoped that the Bad Man was not angry with him. The Bad Man frightened the boy. Frightened the boy more than he could have imagined.

The Bad Man had invited the boy into The Pipe and nothing had been the same since. Things were better. The boy felt wanted and had purpose. He had come alive thanks to the Bad Man.

* * *

And then, the boy was walking back into the town with the Bad Man. They were searching. The Bad Man said he was hungry. The boy knew better than to ask what he was hungry for. They would both know when they found it.

It didn't take long. And the Bad Man's choice was as ever, perfect. The boy heard his prey before seeing it. The incessant barking of Mrs Toleman's little shit of a dog. No, not barking. Yapping. That shitty little thing was not a dog. It was a ratty little dog wannabe. The boy would be doing the town a service. He would be doing Mrs Toleman a service. She could go out and get herself a proper dog next time.

The next bit fascinated the boy. All of it fascinated him and more. He had stirrings which he knew were wrong. His Mother had told him about the stirrings and told the boy that they were a sin. The biggest of the sins at that. That his father was a man led by those stirrings and that was why he was no longer in their lives. The boy felt guilt about the stirrings after he was done. The guilt was itself a dirty thing. It gloated and it weighed heavily upon him. And the guilt had his Mother's face. He couldn't stop though. Knew that he wouldn't stop. The Bad Man was his only friend and he wanted only to please the Bad Man. Besides, he enjoyed it. He enjoyed all of it, even the guilty part, and it got better every time they did it.

Mrs Toleman's dog had ceased its incessant yapping. This was part of the fascination. When their prey saw the Bad Man they were filled with a curious brand of fear. They knew that the Bad Man was terrible and that they were in trouble, but the fear that filled them was somehow calming. They stood still and compliant in a strange form of paralysis and it was easy work for the boy to then take them.

But first, the boy took something out of the bag he carried with him everywhere that he went.

CLICK!

WHIR!

He checked the ratty shit-rat's tag, Smudge. The boy grinned, thinking, you will be a smudge soon enough! He lifted the dog. It's was as though it were a piece of taxidermy. He walked back to the forest and The Pipe with the small dog under his arm. No one saw him. No one ever saw him. And no one ever saw the Bad Man, unless the Bad Man wanted them to see him, and then he would be the last thing that they ever saw.

* * *

Shut!

THE PIPE

The gate was shut!

A terror gripped Charlie. If the gate really was shut then they were in all sorts of trouble.

A secondary thought; who had shut the gate? And where was the person who shut the gate?

The torch was swinging wildly as they half walked and half jogged towards the gate. Charlie could not see the gate properly. She was looking for that chain. If the chain was padlocked around that gate then they were stuck here in The Pipe with that thing and it was game over.

Then the torch flickered and the light dimmed.

"No!" they all cried. They could not countenance the light dying. They did not know what they would do if the torch died.

"Kabir! The batteries are going!" shouted Archie.

Kabir did not answer. That was answer enough. There were no replacement batteries and they did not have a second torch. This was it. This was all they had, and it looked like they wouldn't have it for much longer.

The torch did not linger. It did not afford them a dimmer light for the remainder of their return walk out of The Pipe. It dimmed. It dimmed some more. And then they were in the pitch black. Behind a closed gate.

In the total darkness, Kabir walked into Archie's back.

"Hey!" Archie protested.

Charlie slowed, and despite anticipating Kabir's stationary body, she bumped gently into his back. Kabir said nothing. He understood that it was an accident and that Charlie was doing her best.

"The gate?" asked Charlie in a quiet voice, noticing the desperation and fear contained in those two words.

"I'm trying!" snapped Archie who was now frantically scrabbling at the gate.

There was a crash and crack and the sound of something smashing.

"Hey! My torch!" protested Kabir as he realised what the sound was.

"It's useless!" countered Archie.

"It's my Dad's! He'll kill me!" Kabir was indignant and upset at his friend.

Archie laughed. It was not a kind laugh. It was cruel and bitter, "He can't kill you if you're already dead! And thanks to your torch, we're all going to die down here."

The three children fell silent as one of them felt around the gate attempting to remember what it looked like and what it was that he was looking for. It took what felts like an age before he found the handle on the bolt.

"Yes!" he exclaimed as his hand wrapped around the handle. Then he pulled. The bolt did not budge, "Help me!" he commanded and Kabir scrabbled around, eventually finding his friend's hands, he joined in the effort to pull.

Nothing. The bolt would not budge.

"Wait!" said Charlie, "give me some room."

There was something in her voice. Kabir and Archie felt her brush past them. Even Archie dared not speak up. Charlie had taken over right now and in any case, he was happy to relinquish leadership in these dire moments.

"Step back a bit," she said more quietly. Both of the boys complied.

Charlie had hold of the edge of the gate with her left hand and with her right she had hold of the edge of the frame. She braced and she pulled. She was right. The heavy gate moved, ever so slowly. It was heavy and unyielding. This was not the same gate that they breezed through earlier. That gate had wanted to admit entry. Wanted them to venture deeper into The Pipe. This gate performed a different purpose. This gate does not want them to leave.

"Help me pull this open!" Charlie gasped.

Kabir knew straight away what needed to be done. And he reached out, finding the gate in the dark and joined in, helping his friend to pull the gate open. Archie seemed frozen. Bewildered.

"Archie!" shouted Charlie, urgency in her voice. This would take all three of them. Without Archie, the gate would not open. He snapped out of his fugue and reached out. He was clumsy and he hit Kabir in his clumsiness before lending his weight with that of the gate.

"No!" Charlie and Kabir cried out in unison and this rallied them all. Archie grabbed the gate and as he pulled, as the other two redoubled their efforts, the gate slowly opened.

Charlie realised that they would not have long. As soon as they let go, the gate would swing back shut. The three of them needed to time this right, and get out through the gate before it closed shut on them. If it did. Whoever was stuck behind that gate would not come through it. Not ever.

For something was coming for them and they didn't have much time left. No time at all.

"We need to get out through this gate quickly and together," Charlie was panting with the effort of holding the gate open. She sensed the other two nodding. Wanted to laugh at the ridiculousness of nodding in the pitch black, but she knew that if she were to start laughing she might not stop, that right now she was so close to unravelling that she had to be very careful. They were all close to losing themselves and each other down here in the dark. They needed each other and right now, Archie and Kabir needed Charlie, "On three," she said calmly.

One.

Two.

Three.

There was movement and gasps and Charlie felt herself falling. Someone partially landed on her, but that was alright. That was more than alright.

"Kabir?" she said softly into the darkness.

"Yes," said the owner of the leg and arm that were sprawled on Charlie. He moved. Managed to grab Charlie's face.

"Ow!" she yelped.

"Sorry!" Kabir apologised.

They both found their feet. "You OK?" asked Charlie.

"I think so," answered Kabir.

They went quiet. Archie had said nothing. The ebullient Archie had not said a word.

There was a soft, muted noise. Charlie focused on it. Moved towards it. The sound she could hear was gentle sobbing. This was at least something. They could work with something she thought and she tried not to think about the circumstances under which sobbing was a very bad thing. What she couldn't help thinking was whether that sobbing was on the wrong side of a closed shut gate. A closed gate that she knew would not open. If Archie was on the wrong side of that gate, then it would never open again for him. This Charlie knew. She didn't know how she knews it, and that added to the terrible feeling she had right now.

She shuffled towards the noise of the sobbing.

"Archie?" she asked cautiously.

The sobbing almost stopped, then it dropped back into its former rhythm. He had heard her. That was good wasn't it? She crouched and reached down. Breathed a breath of relief and thanked The Lord. Archie was on this side of the gate. What if he was caught in the gate though? What if part of him was broken and crushed in the gate?

She moved her hand around trying to find his hand. He was limp and motionless. He hardly reacted as Charlie found his hand and slipped her fingers into his.

"Come on," she said reassuringly as she straighted up and pulled him up with her.

Archie began to come with her. They were going to be OK. They were going to be OK! Despite everything. Despite the complete darkness and the evil in this place, they had gotten through that damned gate and they were going to get out of here.

Archie stopped. Charlie pulled, but there is no give.

"I'm stuck!" Archie was panicked and pleading.

Charlie kicked herself for tempting providence. It was almost too easy. She thought they'd done it, but of course they hadn't. It was never going to be that easy.

Charlie took a deep breath and asked a question that she wasn't sure she wanted an answer to. A voice in her head was already repeating over and over...

What are we going to do?

What are we going to do?

What are we going to do?

It wasn't a question, it was a chant. It was a chant that had one purpose and one purpose only. To drive Charlie mad. To fill her with panic which then gave way to a myriad other feelings that would smash her to pieces inside.

"Where are you stuck?" asked Charlie.

There was a pause. It's bad, thought Charlie. Really bad.

"My coat!" whined Archie.

"Your…" For a second time, Charlie wanted to laugh.

"Take it off!" hissed Kabir.

Good old Kabir, thought Charlie. She wanted to thank him, but knew that this would make Archie angry. He'd see it as undermining him and the other two ganging up against him and he just couldn't take that, especially in his current, compromising position.

"No!" Archie was indignant.

"You have to!" hissed Kabir again.

"My Mum'll kill me!" protested Archie.

"That makes two of us then," Kabir said through gritted teeth, "Charlie can put flowers on both our graves."

There was a deep sigh from behind Archie and this time the stench was terrible. It was the belch of a corpse and the three children should not have understood that. They sensed movement. There really as something coming for them. They had to get out of here now.

"Archie!" Charlie whispered urgently.

Archie was fumbling and furiously wriggling.

A sound closer to them.

"Come on!" urged Kabir and something in his voice made Charlie think he was going to run. She reached out instinctively and grabbed his hand. Felt Kabir pull. Knew that had she not got his hand then he would have gone. He would have left them and damn the consequences.

"Archie!" Charlie spoke firmly. They had to go right now.

Archie whined. There was a tearing noise and then he was right next to Charlie. The sobbing had started again. She found his hand and this time, he squeezed hers and he did not let go. Would not let go.

"Let's go," Charlie said quietly towards Kabir and they walked steadily but surely along The Pipe. Archie quietly sobbing.

They hadn't got far when there was a crash of metal against metal.

The sudden noise in the oppressive silence made all three of them start,

3

Archie crushed Charlie's hand and it was all she could do not to cry out.

"Keep going!" she hissed, "It was the gate slamming shut again."

That sounded right. They hadn't heard the gate slam shut as they themselves had gone through it had they? Archie had probably been caught on the frame.

Whatever the truth of it was, it no longer mattered.

There was a howl of rage. A terrible noise which crashed along the confining walls and reverberated. It was the sound of a man, but it was more than that. Whatever was behind them wasn't human. Not anymore.

They ran.

Keeping hold of each other's hands. They ran for their lives.

Another howl. Further away this time.

Charlie thought that whatever it was that had followed them was stuck behind the gate. But they had left it unbolted hadn't they? In their haste to leave they had not bolted the gate. They had unbolted it on the way in, and now? Now it was open. Charlie thought this was important. You never left gates open or unbolted. If you did, then things could get out and that always ended badly.

They couldn't stop now though. Their lives depended on them getting out of here and getting out of here now.

As they neared the end of The Pipe, had to be nearing the end of The Pipe despite the absence of daylight. Charlie remembered the sense of being watched. Watched by the forest. This part of the forest was enchanted, but some enchantment was evil. The forest called to people and watched as they were fed to The Pipe. Charlie knew that now. This place was ancient and evil and they were lucky to have a chance to get away. There was the other thing watching them though. Something had been in the forest watching them. What if it was still out there?

* * *

THE PIPE

The boy walked with purpose towards the forest. As he got closer to the tree line he seemed to straighten and grow. This was his purpose. This was his reason for being. He felt bigger and better. This empowered him and he could feel energy coursing within him. An electric charge that was building as he approached The Pipe. He would unleash himself upon this animal and he would show everyone who he really was. He was powerful and his power grew every time he took a life. Soon, ratty little shit-dogs would not be enough. Soon he would take bigger prey and his power would know no bounds.

The boy strode into the forest and made his way through the more widely used part of the woodland. Here, the dog walkers took their dogs and children had adventures. This part of the forest was safe. He passed around the clearing, seemingly avoiding it and sticking to the dappled light under the trees, and went into his place. This part of the forest was dense and unwelcoming. It was also not part of the publicly owned woodland. This was privately owned, but the fences and signs had long ago degraded, collapsed and become overgrown. The ownership of this land dated back centuries and no one was quite sure who it was that now owned this corner of the forest.

If anyone were to have encountered the boy as he neared The Pipe they would have stopped in their tracks. There was something off about him. The bewildered and silent dog under his arm was bad enough. The unwavering stare of his eyes, forever focused on The Pipe and nothing else was unnerving. The terrible, blood specked rictus grin frightening. In the light of dusk though, there was a shadow behind the boy that pulsed darker with every step he took towards The Pipe. With each pulse, there was a glimpse of a dark figure. Now that he was in the private forest, the Big Man rose up and out of the boy and as The Pipe came into sight the pulsing was no longer discernible. The Big Man was there, he loomed large and the forest welcomed its master back.

The Pipe awaited its master.

There was something terrible about the silent dog. It did not even whimper as a look of recognition and resignation flickered across its face.

3

The boy did not slow as he strode into The Pipe.

The sound of steps echoed out from darkness within The Pipe.

Soon, the screeching of a gate being shouldered open was to be heard.

Here, the boy paused. He reached down and picked something up from the ground. A coat. It fell open as he lifted it, revealing an inner pocket with a label on it. On the label was writ; Archie Bates.

The boy raised the coat to his nose and inhaled. He knew Archie Bates and he knew the other two, Kabir Vanga and Charlie Jones. They went to his school. He'd seen them. And now he'd seen them in his special place. They would pay for their insolence, for coming here. He would make them pay.

He straightened. Now he had work to do and it would not wait. He dragged the coat behind him as he walked to the end of the tunnel.

It wasn't the end of The Pipe though. The Pipe went much further than this. This was where the boy made his sacrifices and learnt his trade. There was a skill to *unmaking* that the boy was learning quickly. At first he was clumsy and he had displeased the Bad Man. The sacrifices died too quickly. They died too easily. Now though, the boy could unmake an animal and make it last for a long time. A very long time indeed. There was a skill to this and the reward for his growing skill was pleasure.

With this one, the boy would unmake to a point that would leave the ratty shit holding onto its unworthy life until he came back to finish it off. The Bad Man fed on pain as well as the life force of the sacrifice. The boy had learnt this and it was a skill he needed to continue to hone so he could enjoy the bigger kills and the ultimate sacrifices fully. The boy had to be ready and he had to be worthy.

All of this was a build up. The anticipation of what this was all leading to made him salivate. He was dribbling as he cast Archie's coat onto the pile of dead decomposing and unmade animals. He breathed deeply of them as he placed the small dog in front of them. It gave one quiet and low whimper as it felt a claw brush it's neck. The boy and the Bad Man would take their time. They would play and they would delay the onset of the pain. He sank a claw inwards and was rewarded with a squeal of surprise and anguish. Pinning the small animal there with that claw he brandished the others, showing the

animal the manner of its death. Wails of pain echoed along the walls of The Pipe, together with other terrible sounds and flashes of red light.
CLICK!
WHIR!

* * *

Something was looking after Charlie, Kabir and Archie that day, not that they knew it or appreciated it. As they emerged from The Pipe the light of the summer's day was fading, but they had enough to see by. They walked quickly through the forest, not slowing for anything. Oblivious to their surroundings, the branches whipping and scratching them, but they did not care. All that mattered was getting home.

As they burst through into the clearing they had set out from, at a time which seemed an age away, not earlier that very same day, they were unaware of the boy as he walked nearby. For their part, the boy and the Bad Man were unaware of the three children, so intent were they upon returning to The Pipe and feeding. So they passed each other without seeing or encountering the other party.

Not long after, the three children spilled out onto the pavement on the outer edge of the forest. They were back and they were safe in the humdrum world of the suburbs and the housing estate that they all lived on.

Only now did they allow themselves to relax. As they did, they felt the last of their energy leave them. They were done in and not relishing the prospect of the last leg of the journey home.

They stood around each other. Not quite knowing what to do next. Perhaps not wanting to part because deep down, they knew that this was a goodbye of sorts. That after they parted, they would never be the same again. Something had happened to them in The Pipe and the curse would begin wreaking its pain and misery as soon as they walked their separate ways. Parting would make it all the more real.

Kabir noticed Archie's arm. From it was hanging the remnants of his coat, "You're coat…" he said redundantly.

Archie scowled at him and pulled what was left of the arm of his coat off and flung it petulantly into the nearby bushes.

"You've…" said Kabir.

Charlie followed Kabir's line of sight and her heart sank. She wished she could take what Kabir had said back. He had spoken without thinking and he also wished that he hadn't said anything.

Archie had wet himself. It was a miracle that neither Charlie nor Kabir had, they had all three of them lost it back there.

Tears welled in Archie's eyes. Tears of shame and anger. He bunched his fists, and barely contained himself. Maybe seeing the look on Kabir's face prevented him from lashing out at his friend; he was so, so sorry. He hadn't meant to say anything. He wished with all his heart that he could take it back. He hadn't thought to take their expedition into The Pipe back, that was how important Archie and his friendship was to Kabir.

It was too late though, the damage was done. Archie would turn his shame and anger on Kabir and on Charlie. He would blame them and he would distance himself from them. It was an excuse and he knew it. An easy focal point that masked the real reason for his pain. The Pipe.

Archie turned and stomped off.

Kabir called after him, "Archie! I'm sorry!"

Archie did not turn. He did not even slow.

Kabir made to run after his friend. Charlie caught his arm and held him, "leave him, Kabir. He needs to be alone right now." She would wonder whether that was the right call. Should they both have run after him and sorted it out there and then? She would never be sure on this score, but she knew one thing. You could never take it back. You could never go back and change a thing. Life was cruel like that, it gave you one chance, but it didn't tell you when the chance was or how important it was going to be. You only found out after you had rolled the dice and it had all unfolded around you.

Kabir didn't argue. The fight quickly left him. They walked quietly together until they reached the turn for Kabir's road. He mumbled a quiet goodbye and left Charlie to walk the short distance to her own house. She made to walk away. Walked a few steps. Stopped. Watched Kabir's retreating back. Knowing it might be the last time she saw him like this. That maybe their friendship would not survive what had happened in The Pipe. That it could not survive something like this.

4

Something had changed.

The three of them knew it and it was obvious to others.

The three amigos were no longer as tight as they had been. There was an almost tangible distance between them and none of them ever crossed it. They didn't know how, because somewhere in the middle of that distance was The Pipe. It was worse for Archie because he had disgraced himself and he judged others by his own standards. Had Charlie known this, she would have spoken to him and told him it was alright. The problem was Archie wouldn't have been able to bear even that. Charlie or Kabir reassuring him was too much to take, because they would *still* be talking about what he had done. They would be using it against him and they would always have the upper hand; Archie had cried and he had peed himself. Archie was a little pant pissing cry baby and he couldn't look at Charlie or Kabir again, not without seeing his own, abject failure.

Maybe without Archie, Charlie and Kabir could have continued to be friends and perhaps, had they managed to bridge the gap between them they could have eventually brought Archie back into the fold. It was not to be though. The Pipe was ever present. It haunted them. The alure that it had once had had turned to poison. It had forever stained them and it lurked in their dreams, turning them to nightmares. Again and again they would glimpse a carnal house of mutilated creatures and something more terrible than that.

Him.

The Bad Man.

THE PIPE

Children grow up though and they cope with change. They are built to. They have a resilience that grown-ups under estimate and it is just as well, because when tragedy strikes, grown-ups are caught in the midst of it, in their own grief and try as they might, they don't give all that much to their children. They can't. They themselves are broken, in pain and unable to see clearly. In pain, they revert to their basic, selfish ways.

Tragedy was approaching one of the households of the three children and that tragedy would fracture their friendship even further.

* * *

The Sun had been true to her word. She had done her job well and she'd stuck around far into September. When she left, she left an absence and the inhabitants of the town missed her. The cold came in on a Northerly wind and cut right through them. There was a promise of snow on that wind and a hard winter was mustering its armies even now.

The days got shorter as well as colder and a gloom began to descend upon the town and its people. The children stayed outside and they played. Eking out as much time outdoors as they possibly could. Archie and Kabir found new people to hang out with. It wasn't the same, but they got on with things and tried not to think about what their former friends were doing. In their hearts, they were still friends. They convinced themselves they were taking some sort of break. That everything would be OK. They were learning to be adults and as they'd seen, adults became very adept at lying to themselves.

Charlie stayed home a lot more. She found other things to occupy her mind. She read several times a day and she had learnt the game of chess, so she played and she read chess books and practiced on a mini chess computer that she took everywhere with her.

On the day in question, she was in her room, a chess set on her bedside table and a book on her lap. That was when she heard the scream. At first she could not place it. Such a sound did not belong in this house and it didn't

4

seem real. It didn't seem human.

The scream went on and on and then it gave way to a keening sound punctuated by more, intermittent screams.

The sound was unnerving and frightening, the pitch jangled the teeth in Charlie's face. On leaden feet she crept quietly from her room and came part way down the stairs. She could see her Mum's back and in front of her Mum was her Dad. He was carrying something in his arms that Charlie could not see as her Mum was obscuring her view.

"He was in the woods," her Dad said in a cracked voice that was not his own.

Charlie sat down heavily on the stairs and her world jarred sideways. It would never go back to where it had been. Her world would forever be off-track from this day forth.

Billy. Her brother. Billy was the *thing* in her Dad's arms and her Mum was screaming because he...

He'd been in the woods.

He'd been in the woods and he was dead.

The Pipe.

Charlie had thought of little else since they had been inside The Pipe.

Now it had done this.

The Pipe had come into their home and it had taken her brother, Billy.

* * *

Charlie didn't know how she had come to no longer be on the stairs and in her bed. No one said anything. In the scheme of things, it wasn't important. What was and wasn't important didn't matter anymore.

Billy was dead.

And it was Charlie's fault.

Charlie was forever marked by The Pipe and The Pipe had seen Billy and taken him.

Charlie's friendship with Archie and Kabir may have been fractured, but now her world was shattered.

Eventually, her Mum stopped screaming. They gave her drugs to help her, but Charlie wondered at that. The drugs seemed to be to shut her up. To stop the screaming. They numbed her Mum so thoroughly that there was nothing left.

Her Mum was still screaming inside though. The drugs just put her on mute while the terrible and awful film of the tragedy of her dead Billy played on. It played over and over and over and each re-run of the film took another piece of her Mum away. Charlie could see it happening. Somehow her silence made it all the more terrifying. To see someone come apart like that. To see her Mum deconstructed.

And it was Charlie's fault, but she couldn't tell anyone and she couldn't make it right. None of it.

Her Dad was no better, but he didn't need the drugs to be numb, he could do that all by himself.

When Billy died, so did something more than Billy. Their home was no longer a home. Charlie's parents retreated within themselves and she was left alone.

Billy had been in the forest. No one knew why. He'd wandered off from the garden and no one had seen him go.

A dog walker found him off the beaten path. He was scratched and bruised, but that wasn't what had killed him.

His neck was broken.

The assumption was that he had tried to climb a tree and had fallen.

Charlie knew different.

So too did two other kids at her school.

The funeral was horrible. Charlie didn't understand most of it and she sat through it watching her parents falling apart all over again.

Neither of her parents blamed Charlie for not being there for her brother, they didn't have to. She did that all by herself. What she didn't get was that she was mirroring what her Mum and Dad were doing. They blamed themselves and a small part of them blamed each other.

4

None of them said anything, so the pain festered and the chance to heal was cast aside.

At Christmas, her Mum said she was taking Charlie to her parents with her. Her Dad didn't say anything in response to this, he just nodded. When it came time to leave, her Dad hugged her harder than he'd ever hugged Charlie before. He held onto her as though he never wanted to let her go. She returned the hug fiercely, fighting the overwhelming urge to cry.

In the car, she waved him goodbye and tried to smile, but couldn't as she saw him crying for the first time in her life.

They never returned home and her Mum got a divorce and moved on with her life.

The town held too many painful memories and she would never go back. There was nothing to go back for. Charlie's Dad hung himself in their old house on the first anniversary of Billy's death.

5

TWENTY YEARS LATER

Some days, you just know that something is coming.

Charlie felt it coming. It wasn't just that she had had a particularly bad night's sleep. That wasn't unusual, she'd not slept well since she was ten. She supposed it predated the day that Billy died, but Billy's passing eclipsed everything else, so she thought that it was *around then*.

Friday nights were a better night for her when it came to sleep. The working week was over and she could rest that bit easier. She was also at her most tired then. The week took it out of her and there was precious little left in the tank when it came to Friday night. She'd begun to cry off social engagements on a Friday night. It wasn't that she didn't want to, or that she wasn't up to it. On the night, she could mix it with the best of them.

It was the morning after that was the problem, or rather that this had extended into the weekend after. Morning after was what it had been, before her powers of recovery had deserted her. Now, she was fragile throughout Saturday, and Sunday was only incrementally better.

So now, at the tender age of thirty, she tried to take it easy on Fridays. She'd show her face sometimes, to show willing, but tried to avoid even that. The temptation to linger and have another drink was too great.

Sleep had taken her last night. She was dog tired. She awoke around three and lay there staring at the ceiling, cursing herself for not being asleep and almost laughing at her own behaviour – winding herself up like that was not going to see her find sleep any time soon.

5

After a while, Charlie realised that she'd not slept well prior to this. She recalled fitful tossing and turning and numerous occasions where she must have awakened, but then rolled over and attempted to get back to sleep. Something had invaded her dreams, she was sure of it, but what it was, she did not know.

At some point, she must have drifted off for a while.

And she was back there. In The Pipe. She knew where she was the instant she opened her eyes. That was the thing. She opened her eyes and she was there. No prelude, no build up or foreplay, she was there. For a moment she thought she was reliving her one and only time in The Pipe. She felt smaller. But then she felt the chair underneath her. She was sitting on a chair in The Pipe. There was a faint light that made everything all the more eerie. Breathing. She could hear breathing. Her own and... there was someone else in The Pipe with her.

Charlie tried to move and this was when she found that she was bound. Tied to the chair. She struggled against her bonds and the seat of the chair moved from side to side. The chair she was sat upon was an office, swivel chair. Establishing this terrified her. The choice of chair was very deliberate. And now she knew what she had her back to. She was at the very end of The Pipe and whoever was with her intended turning her. Turning her to face the nightmare she had glimpsed twenty years ago, only this time she would see it all and she didn't think she could deal with that. She couldn't survive that.

A dark and strange voice spoke in her dream, "I have waited a long time for you, Charlie."

Then a high pitched, and somehow odd, childlike voice began to mutter what sounded like an incantation, only she recognised the words as they were repeated.

...row your boat
Row, row, row.
Row, row, row.
Row, row, row.
If you see a crocodile!

CLICK!
WHIR!
Row, row, row.
Row, row, row.
Row, row, row.
HE'S COMING FOR YOU!
HE'S COMING FOR YOU ALL!
The Bad Man.

Terrible, high pitched laughter. A hand on the back of the chair. Pressure. The chair began to turn towards the horrors that awaited her...

Charlie was sat upright in her bed. Sat, not wanting to turn. Hands bunched into fists. Chords of muscle rising up on her neck. She was gasping. Protesting, "No! No! NO!"

It took her a while to realise that she was in her bedroom. No longer in The Pipe. Her trip to The Pipe had been so real.

Light was battling it's way in around the curtains. She checked the time.
5.58

Decided there was no point in attempting to sleep again. She did not want to return to that dream in any case. She mustered the energy to climb out of bed, her sleep deprived limbs slow to respond. Padding to the bathroom, she absently cleaned her teeth and then stepped into the shower. The initial jet of cool water helping to wake her up. She spent a while under the cascading water, allowing it to cleanse her, hoping it would wash away the bad night, or at least the best part of it.

The dog began howling and barking half-heartedly as she exited the shower. He wanted her to know that he was still here. That he'd been waiting for her and now she needed to know that she had kept him long enough. As far as he was concerned, she was to hurry down here right now and give him a fuss which he'd be too excited to really notice or appreciate. Then he wanted to run out into the garden and have a word with the birds. They were encroaching on his territory and that just would not do. In all the confusion, he hoped that he would remember to go to the toilet, but there was the small matter of his breakfast and that took precedence. When he'd eaten he would go to the toilet. Then he'd drink some water. Then a walk! He really wanted a walk! Then a fuss until he was asleep where he would sleep soundly, dreaming of chasing rabbits. Only to wake up again and demand fuss. Sleep, excitement, fuss and the all-important meals and walks. That was her dog's life.

Charlie obliged the dog. It was the least she could do and it was their routine. In return, the dog filled the house with his presence and just a little bit of dirt and mess. The deal worked for them both and it made Charlie and Shap's house a home. Charlie needed Shap and Shap loved her to bits. He barked to tell her this, then nudged her hard with his nose, then he followed her so closely to the back door that she would have been tripped by him had she not learned long ago to take short steps and allow for his exuberance.

The coffee was poured and Charlie was awaiting the toast's leap from the toaster as she sipped from her mug and stared vacantly out of the window. She couldn't shake the feeling that there was something out of whack. That the day had started all wrong and that it wasn't going to get any better. That this was the high point and the only way from here was down.

The dog's hackles rose and he growled, his whole body suddenly alert. Muscles tought as he stared warily towards the front door. Charlie patted Shap and told him to stop being silly. It was the second time she had ever seen him like this and it spooked her.

Today it spooked her badly.

The toast chose this moment to pop up. The sudden sound and movement made Charlie jump. Shap barked, more alarmed by Charlie's reaction to the toast than the toast itself. There was a rattle as something was pushed in through the letterbox. Shap's growl slipped into a whine. He scampered away, tail between his legs, he crawled under the table. His safe space and a place he seldom used.

Charlie watched him go, wondering what had gotten into him. She turned to the door, something held her back. Usually, she would be excited at the prospect of post, even when bitter experience told her it was likely bills and junk mail. She glanced in the direction Shap went, wanting to follow him. Part of her didn't want to see what it was that was now laying on her door mat. Waiting for her.

She shook herself. Telling herself not to be so silly. What could possibly harm her? She was in her own home and she was safe. Someone had posted something through the letterbox was all.

Still, Charlie hung back. Toast forgotten. She watched through the window for whoever had made the delivery. No one emerged from the blind spot by her front door. She rationalised that she must have been distracted by Shap and missed them. This helped her snap out of her hesitancy and she hoped, the strange mood brought on by lack of sleep. She was also curious in case whoever had made the delivery was lingering by the front door. Perhaps they also had a parcel and had not pressed the doorbell properly.

She went to the front door. There on the mat was a single rectangle of white card. She eyed it warily, reluctant to stoop down and pick it up.

"Why are you being such a wuss!?" she said to herself quietly.

It was after all, only a piece of card. Likely a postcard advertising a local old folks' home or replacement windows. Something to barely glance at and then drop into the recycling bin. Charlie hoped that she was doing the right thing and that her junk mail was being recycled, or else, what was the point? It was all that it was good for.

She picked it up carefully. It shook between her fingers. Charlie realised that it shook because she was shaking, she was thrumming in something like a cold and fearful anticipation. The address was written in childlike writing. The addressee: Charlie. Set out like a postcard, the name and address on the right hand side and a short message on the left hand side:

To Charlie,

Wish you were here.

The Bad Man

Something caught in her throat as she read the message and who it was from. Her hand shook even more fiercely now and she let out a barely audible, strangled cry. She dared not turn the card to see what was on the other side. Part of her dream came unbidden to her now. A sound she had heard before, on that fateful day twenty years ago, just as they were about to enter The Pipe.

5

CLICK!
WHIR!

The card, it had that shiny, smooth feel. She thought she knew what was on the other side. She turned it over slowly and carefully, her heart beating rapidly.

The card was a polaroid photo, and as she turned it to reveal the image on the other side, she saw that it was them. It was Archie. It was Kabir. And it was Charlie. The photo captured them twenty years ago as they stood around the mouth of The Pipe, about to venture in and make the biggest mistake in their young lives. She shivered. Someone had been there watching them and that someone had taken their photo. Twenty years on, they'd sent the photo and this message.

Why now?

Charlie was sat at her kitchen table, drinking her now barely warm coffee whilst staring at the photo of her and her two best friends. Her eyes were red and raw as though she had been crying, but no tears would come. She'd rubbed at her eyes absently as she sat there. Tears would have been tears of self-pity. She couldn't change the past.

She could never change the past.

The past.

She picked up her phone and tapped on the calendar app. It must be twenty years almost to the day. Perhaps the sender of the photo was marking the anniversary? She picked the photo up and turned it in her hands. No stamp or postmark. This had been delivered by hand. How did they know she lived here? Had they come all the way here from her old home town?

The old legend, *wish you were here* was the only message.

What did it mean?

Her phone buzzed. She picked it up to see who had messaged her.

Kabir.

That was a blast from the past! The last time they had… It had never been the same after they'd entered The Pipe. Then Billy had died. Charlie didn't remember much from that time, she supposed that Kabir and Archie had been at the funeral. She knew that she had been there, but so numb and uncomprehending as not to be there. That was what they meant when someone was *out of it*. She'd been so out of it as to be nowhere at all. Entombed in a dark limbo that was frighteningly familiar.

Her finger hovered over the unopened message. Delaying. What did Kabir want? Why was he contacting her out of the blue. Yes, they were friends on social media, but these days that meant very little at all. You could have hundreds of friends on there and hear regularly and meaningfully from only a handful. The majority of social media users stuck to posting the same old crap that gave nothing away about them and how they were. Then there were the voyeurs, users who seldom posted online, but liked to visit and see what others were posting.

Few people ever genuinely gave of themselves. Less so online.

Charlie realised that she was distracting herself with tangential thoughts about the use of social media, why did she not want to open Kabir's message? She thought she knew – when someone hasn't meaningfully spoken to you in a decade or more, then drops you a note out of the blue, then it's nearly always going to be bad news. Someone has died, Charlie tought to herself. Kabir is contacting me to tell me...

It's Archie.

A lead weight dropped into her insides and her head swam. She was looking at the photo again. At the three of them. The photo. Archie. She pressed Kabir's message.

The message was long. It began with an apology. Been too long. Where do the years go. Sorry to approach you like this and be the bearer of bad news.

Archie.

Charlie heard herself sob. Felt detached from the sound and herself.

Archie was dead.

Archie was dead and the past she had done her best to bury was back in the forefront of her life. It had never left her. It would never leave her.

6

Archie's funeral was a lacklustre affair, but then this was Charlie's view of funerals. The horse had bolted and those remaining were staring at the gate. Trying to do something to mark someone's passing. A final gesture which would never be seen by the departed.

Better to have made the effort while the deceased was still alive. Charlie should have done something. She should have reached out to Archie, and now it was too late. And in Archie's inimitable style, he had taken control and had the last word. The onus was left with Charlie, she should have reached out, how could Archie when he was too busy with the business of dying before either of his friends?

Archie's farewell was particularly poignant thanks to the intimate number of guests, some of which looked to be a part of the church the funeral took place in. Nothing made sense to Charlie when it came to this part of someone's life, but that there was not a big crowd to see the gregarious Archie off was a shock for her.

Kabir nodded at Charlie at the graveside and once the ceremony had concluded she joined him as he walked back towards his car.

"Where's the wake?" she asked as she caught up with him.

"Hello Charlie," something like sarcasm and weariness in Kabir's voice.

"Sorry, hi Kabir," Charlie shrugged as Kabir stopped to face her, "I've never been good at these things."

Kabir looked about to say something, remembered something and thought better of it, "Yeah, me neither." His turn to shrug, "there's no wake. This is it."

Charlie looked back at the graveside. The few other attendees had already dispersed and gone. She returned her gaze to Kabir. Puzzled and disappointed.

Was this it?

"Listen," Kabir fished in his pocket and retrieved a bundle of keys which he jangled in front of him, "I've got a lot to tell you, so let's go back to his house. Drop our cars off. There's a pub nearby."

Charlie nodded. She could do with a drink right now, "OK, I'll follow you there."

Kabir nodded and she walked over to her car. Noting that Kabir's was a brand new, squat, purple, high spec BMW. Her own car a low spec and ageing car that blended in with its surroundings, such was the level of unremarkable it attained.

They drove across the seaside town. Summer should have seen the small town hustling and bustling with visitors, but this place had fallen out of vogue decades ago, when cheap flights to guaranteed sunny destinations had robbed it of its lifeblood. It was still dying a slow and painful death. Even in the heat of a glorious summer's day this place was dull and insipid. It spoke of illness and death. The facades of once grand buildings were decaying and uninviting. The few people who wandered the litter strewn streets looked shell shocked and bewildered. They looked unhealthy and ill. The fight had left them a long time ago.

Charlie looked out at the bleak and broken vista and found herself thinking that it was a place where you came to die. Why had Archie come here? What had happened to him? Why had so few people come to his funeral. What path had his short life taken? They may not have been ten years old anymore, but they were kids still. Charlie knew she still had a lot of growing up to do. Her friend hadn't been given the chance to.

Kabir turned out of the town proper and took a small coastal rode for about half a mile. He was turning into the driveway of a grand Georgian detached house before Charlie had realised that this must be where he was staying. She turned in and go out of her car.

"I thought we were going to Archie's..." she trailed off.

Kabir had the keys in his hand and was walking up the steps to the front

6

door.

This was not a hotel or upmarket B&B, this was Archie's place.

Kabir swung the door wide and waved her in. The hallway was wide and the floor tiled in black and white diagonal check, a bare wooded banister accompanied grand stairs that swept up to the next floor. There was nothing grand about Charlie's place, and yet Archie's pad launched into grandeur as soon as the impressive oak front door swung open.

"This is… was… Archie's place?" Charlie asked in awe.

"It was, but not anymore!" Kabir was jangling the keys and grinning.

"It's yours?" asked Charlie.

"Half of it, yes…"

Charlie paused, examined Kabir's face for any clues, "and the other half?"

"Shall we grab a drink?" asked Kabir delaying the answer to the question, "the pub is a short walk back the way we came."

Charlie nodded, giving him a look so he knew he wasn't off the hook and that she wasn't best pleased at not getting an answer. She watched him turn back towards the door and once she knew he wasn't looking her way her face fell into a partial scowl. He'd just grinned at her gleefully whilst waving the house keys in her face. That was odd behaviour on the day of their friend's funeral wasn't it?

Then again, funerals weren't Charlie's thing and she'd not seen Kabir in an age. She rationalised that strange episode and dismissed it as they left the house and Kabir locked up.

Kabir led the way. Charlie hadn't spotted any pub on the way here, and she was more intent on the sea view as they walked together. There was always something calming and soothing about being near the sea. She could smell the salt in the air. Archie had picked himself a good spot. If you avoided the diseased and dying town and pretended it didn't exist that was.

Kabir was right about the walk being a short one, Charlie was broken out of her sight-seeing reverie, "Charlie?" He was standing by the open door, waiting for her.

THE PIPE

**

"To Archie," Kabir said quietly and sombrely as he raised his glass of gin and tonic.

Charlie raised her own pint of ale, "Archie."

They sat in silence for a while. Tasting their drinks and looking into them. Contemplative. Not necessarily thinking of Archie. Their thoughts had begun there, but then spiralled off wherever thoughts do when death and its opposite number are considered.

Charlie shivered, someone had just walked over her grave. She had a fleeting moment of darkness, almost a prelude to fainting, but it passed as quickly as it arrived. She noticed that Kabir was watching her.

"He left everything to us," Kabir said over his glass. Awkward. Using the glass to hide behind as he told her the news.

Charlie put hers down, "Really?"

"Oh yes," confirmed Kabir, holding his glass still, but lowering it slightly so she could see all his face now.

"Why?"

"You saw the funeral," said Kabir flippantly.

That didn't sit right with Charlie. None of it did. This wasn't the future she had seen for Archie. This version of his future was so far away from anything she would have expected that it made no sense to her at all.

Kabir saw the look on Charlie's face, "He lost his parents while he was at uni. He was an only child. I suppose he bought his place with the inheritance. There's old family photos that look to be holiday's here. The house may even have been in the family and passed down."

"OK, the no family bit I get, Kabir. But friends? Work colleagues?"

"Ah! Now the work bit I can answer and that might answer the friends thing too. He was freelance. A big name in the gaming industry. Did it all from home. You should see the basement, it's a shrine to tech!"

"So he stayed at home and played computer games?" asked Charlie.

"No. He built them!"

6

Charlie looked none the wiser.

"Cyberpunk Zombies? The Stalking Dead? Undead Melee?" Kabir looked agog at Charlie's failure to recognise the titles of popular and trendy games. These were *the* games to play.

Charlie pulled an apologetic face in response, "what can I say? I have a life?" Her face fell at her inappropriate choice of words.

Kabir winked, "there we go! This is a bit more like a wake now isn't it?"

Charlie smiled. Kabir was right. The wakes Charlie had attended as an adult were drunken affairs. Irreverent. Memories were shared and celebrated. Stories recounted and nothing was spared. Wakes made more sense to Charlie. There was something more of the departed in those moments than there ever was at the funeral itself. It was just a shame that the dead were not given some notice so that they could have one last knees up before departing. Wakes would be all the better for that one additional attendee.

Charlie raised her glass, "it's good to see you again, Kabir." And she meant it.

"Likewise," Kabir smiled sadly, "we left it too late for the reunion of the Three Amigos."

Charlie returned his smile.

"What happened to the three of us, Charlie?" asked Kabir, a sadness and slight desperation in his voice. Suddenly grasping after what could have been.

"You know what happened," said Charlie quietly.

This stopped Kabir in his tracks.

Billy.

"Yes, I'm sorry. That was a terrible tragedy…"

"It wasn't that!" Charlie hissed across the table, "It wasn't that and you know it, Kabir!"

Kabir looked hurt. Wouldn't look up at Charlie. Couldn't look her in the eye. "I…" he began, not knowing where his words would lead.

"We should never have gone into that bloody pipe," snapped Charlie, "that's what happened. There was something very bad down there and it broke us.

And then it..." Charlie trailed off, leaving the rest unsaid.

Kabir couldn't argue with this. He had wanted to. Thought he'd gotten over the events of that day. They weren't that bad were they? They'd all got out in one piece. He could feel it though. And recently he'd felt it all the more, he'd returned time and time again to how it had felt when they were in The Pipe, and to the aftermath of what had happened to them on that day. It would never leave him however much he tried to deny it and however much he tried to forget it.

"There's a box..." Kabir began.

Charlie's interest was piqued. Something about the way Kabir had said box. She stared at her old school friend. He looked worried. Worse than that, she now noticed his eyes and a greyness to his complexion that she knew had been there all along, but she'd been too busy to spot.

"Are you OK, Kabir?"

"What?" he looked momentarily startled, "Yes, why?"

"It's just you look exhausted?"

"Oh, that. I've not been sleeping."

"This box?" asked Charlie.

"Yes, it's in the living room. There's a note saying we should open it together."

"And you have no idea what's in it?"

Kabir looked away quickly, "no."

Charlie laughed.

"What?" asked Kabir.

It was amazing that after all these years, Charlie still knew her old friend. The years had just tumbled away in the moment that he'd looked away, "You always were a bad liar, Kabir!"

Kabir sighed, "OK, I've not looked in the box, but I think I know what's in there."

"What?" she asked.

"Let's go and have a look shall we?"

He necked the last of his gin, not waiting for an answer from Charlie.

6

* * *

Charlie had suggested a take out from the pub. Kabir had told her that there was no need, that Archie had left booze in the house, so they could help themselves. It was after all theirs now.

Back at the house, Charlie was surprised and mildly impressed to see that Archie had enough drink to hold several large parties for a guest list of well-practiced lushes. Strange then that he hadn't seemed to have socialised. It was a vast quantity of alcohol for one person to get through. And in the end, he hadn't.

They cracked open a bottle of red and sat on sofas at either side of the coffee table. On the low coffee table was a battered chocolate tin. The kind that was a family Christmas treat decades back when these things were only bought and eaten at Christmas, not the whole year round. Those tins were much larger than the plastic containers that were sold these days. The chocolates had tasted better too, the recipe for chocolate changing over the years to keep the prices low, the problem was that the chocolate ended up tasting cheap. Those big and substantial tins were often retained. They provided a useful storage solution for items that someone wanted to save and keep safe.

Charlie felt a cold chill creep up from her seat and along her back as Kabir lifted the tin to open it.

"Wait!" she almost shouted.

Kabir froze.

"Kabir?"

He nodded slowly.

"You said you thought you knew what was in the tin?"

"Yes, but I hope that I'm wrong." He looked scared as he said this. He looked very scared.

Charlie reached into her inside pocket. She wasn't sure why she had it with her. Why she'd kept it on her since the day she'd found it on her door mat. She felt the familiar smooth surface and carefully lifted it out and held it towards Kabir.

He leant away, as though what she held were somehow contagious. Poisonous. Dangerous.

"Are you expecting something like this?" she asked.

Kabir nodded awkwardly. His entire body was stiff. He had glanced at the polaroid that Charlie was holding but wouldn't now look at it.

"You've received one as well haven't you?"

Now Kabir was shaking his head, "No, not one," his voice seemed close to breaking as he said this.

"More than one?" Charlie said quietly.

Kabir nodded.

"What are yours of, Kabir?" Charlie asked, "and what are the messages?"

Kabir looked at her curiously. Then, for the first time, he looked at her polaroid properly. She was holding it photo side up.

"Fuck!" he gasped.

"What?!" asked Charlie, wondering what it was about the photo that had shocked him.

"Can I?" he asked.

She handed it to him and he looked it over for a good while before speaking, "It's the same photo as I have. This is the first one I got. Same message, only addressed to me."

"So someone sent us the same polaroid?" said Charlie, not quite getting the significance of what Kabir was saying.

"Don't you see?" urged Kabir.

He could tell from the way Charlie reacted that she didn't see.

"It's a polaroid! It's a one off! It can't..."

Now Charlie saw. Recognition lit her face, "fuck!" she whispered.

"Fuck indeed!" agreed Kabir, "and it's perfect. It's not faded over the last twenty years. Because they do, don't they? However you look after them, polaroids don't last. Only this one has..."

Charlie felt sick as she realised something further, "Kabir?"

"Yes?" he asked very quietly, noting the change in Charlie.

"Have you noticed something else about the photo? I've only just realised..."

6

Kabir shook his head.

Charlie remembered that day far too well. Wasn't sure whether Archie or Kabir had heard the noise behind them.

CLICK!

WHIR!

It was the recollection of those sounds that made her look at the photo anew.

"Shit! I should have seen it as soon as I looked at the bloody photo," she laughed a hollow and mirthless laugh, "there's only one place that that photo could have been taken!"

Kabir's eyes widened, "That's not possible!" He looked at the photo again.

The photo had been taken from inside The Pipe.

7

"Shall I?" Kabir's eyes dropped briefly towards the box on his lap. Now that they'd considered Charlie's polaroid and discovered Kabir had its twin, they expected that Archie's box would contain a third, identical polaroid.

Furthermore, following Kabir's revelation of more polaroids, they expected the tin to contain a pile of them.

Charlie knew they should get this over and done with and open the thing that sat on Kabir's lap. It was better to know for sure. She delayed for a heartbeat. A heartbeat that dragged out and promised much more. They didn't have to do this. They could leave the box. Sometimes it was better not to know. No, it was always better to not know. They were the proof of that. They had gone somewhere that they shouldn't and seen things that were not meant for them. Curiosity had killed more than one cat and a bunch of other animals besides. People were supposed to know better.

Nonetheless, Charlie nodded and watched as Kabir opened the box.

Kabir placed the open box back on the table between them. He did this slowly and almost ceremoniously. There, on the top of a pile of polaroids was the third polaroid that matched their own. The impossible polaroid that could not have been taken of them from where it had been taken and a photo that had to be unique. There was no way a polaroid could be replicated like that. Undiminished by the passage of twenty years, three fresh faces, ten year old adventurers stared up at them.

The terrible thing was not that third copy of their polaroid, the terrible thing was the pile of polaroids underneath that copy. Here was a dark

7

promise. The first polaroid was only the beginning. Under this photo they would see where that beginning lead. And this was a gift to them from their dead friend. A gift that they had accepted and couldn't hand back.

Charlie looked from the box to Kabir, "You said you had more than one?"

He nodded.

"How many, Kabir?"

"Two more," said Kabir grimly.

"When did you get those two?"

"Recently," said Kabir dismissively.

"In the last few weeks?"

"Yes, why?" Kabir was more attentive now. Looking from Charlie to the box, "oh shit!"

Charlie nodded, "after Archie died."

She reached into the box and lifted the pile of photos out. She placed them to one side and moved the empty tin onto the floor. Laying the photos out between them like some sort of tarot card reading and as they began studying the photos, they realised that this was exactly what it was. A reading of a future. There were Archie's cards. His future.

The photos had been placed in the tin in the order they had been delivered. They described a journey from one place to another.

Charlie lifted one of the polaroids and examined the other side. The same child like writing. None of the letters joined. Spacing and sizing all over the place. The addressee; Archie. The message was

He is coming for you!

The first photo after the one of the Pipe twenty years ago was a more recent photo of The Pipe. Then a series of places that may or may not have held significance for Archie. The point was that they described the journey from The Pipe to this place, right here where they were sitting. One of the final photos was of the front of this house. The last of the photos was of the interior of Archie's house.

The final photo's message.

He is here!!!

Only Charlie knew it was not the final photo. There were more. There would be photos of Archie. Inside The Pipe.

Kabir and Charlie looked at all of the photos and the short messages on the reverse side. Most told Archie the same thing over and over.

He is coming for you!

Kabir placed a finger on the photo of the hallway just outside the room they were sitting in, "seen this?"

Charlie looked more closely at what he was pointing at. Looked over the other photos, "it's on them all."

"It's the shape we saw that day isn't it?" whispered Kabir.

It was a shadow that appeared on all but the first photo. A shadow of the thing that they had glimpsed on the day that they had gone inside The Pipe.

Charlie nodded. It was him.

It was the Dark Man.

"You said Archie died suddenly, Kabir. How did he die?" Charlie asked.

"I..." Kabir was nervously scratching his nose as he thought of an answer, "I was told it was sudden. I suppose I thought it was a heart attack."

"But you weren't told it was a heart attack?" Charlie was absently sorting through the photos.

"Now I come to think of it, I think I was only told it was sudden," Kabir let out a low breath. "You don't think it's anything to do with these photos do you?"

Charlie raised an eyebrow in answer. Archie had received a series of macabre messages on the back of photos of someone or something approaching. Something that had started twenty years ago had caught up with him and now he was dead. Suddenly dead. Yes, it could have been a heart attack, but that didn't rule out the ultimate cause being this. These polaroids. Archie was only thirty and although living the life of a recluse, Charlie doubted he was ready to die just yet.

"Kabir?" Charlie's voice was low, but carried all the same. There was weight in that one word.

Kabir looked up from the photos. He looked scared. Haunted even.

"That day we went to the end of The Pipe..." said Charlie leaning forward.

"That was a long time ago, Charlie. We were kids!" Kabir was trying to

7

deflect the conversation about The Pipe.

"Something happened though didn't it?" Kabir could see that Charlie wasn't going to stop, she was determined to have this conversation.

"We were kids with over active imaginations, Charlie. Look at us! We even call that place The Pipe!"

"That's what it is though isn't it?" Charlie sighed, "it's not left me, Kabir. It's in my dreams. And now this. And you've had more of these things," she was pointing at the photos on the table between them.

"It could just be a weirdo couldn't it? A bloody coincidence! Archie died of a…" Kabir sounded like the kid he had been. The kid Charlie would always see. Twenty years had passed, but they were essentially the same. This thing had gotten between them and broken them apart, now it had brought them back together again, albeit Archie was dead so there were only the two of them now.

Charlie didn't answer Kabir's question. They both knew that it wasn't just some weird person, or that if it was, then this particular weirdo was dangerous and not to be ignored.

She pursued the subject she wanted to talk with Kabir about, "what did you see at the end of The Pipe, Kabir?" she asked softly.

Kabir shifted uneasily in his seat, not looking directly at Charlie, but his gaze fell upon the photos and their dark, threatening messages. Messages initially intended for Archie, but messages that were for all three of them. He was coming for them. There really was no doubt about that.

Kabir cleared his throat as Charlie awaited an answer. He glanced at her, quickly looking away from her iron stare. He knew this Charlie. Determined. She wasn't going to take no for an answer, "I saw *him*," he mumbled.

Charlie nodded, this was good. But they had all seen him. That was as much as anyone had ever said. There was someone there. Someone dark. A man. The Bad Man. It was a collective memory and in some ways Charlie could dismiss what Kabir had said. They had all agreed this memory. Maybe Kabir hadn't seen a man. He may have thought he'd seen something and the conviction of the others had led him to backfill his memory with the Bad Man.

"What else, Kabir?"

Kabir shifted about uncomfortably. He really didn't want to go back there. Looked poised to say as much, but then slumped defeated. He spoke, "It was horrible Charlie. Truly horrible. I've never seen anything like it and I have never been able to get it out of my head!" he slapped his temples agitatedly, "I don't know what you guys saw, we never really spoke about it. Then we just didn't speak. Lost touch didn't we?"

Kabir looked up at Charlie imploringly. True sadness and regret in his eyes and a question between them; why *did* we lose touch? He went on, "I only saw it for a moment as the torch beam lit it all up, but that was enough. It was death. It... I'd say it was like an abattoir, but this was worse wasn't it? Animals cut up and... they were arranged! It was like it was some sort of twisted art installation! I think it was a fucked up shrine to *Him*. Someone was killing animals and leaving them for the Bad Man."

Kabir shook his head as though to clear it. Looked across the small table to Charlie, "Is that what you saw, Charlie?" the same sad and regretful look. Pleading for her to say something. To corroborate what he had seen and reassure him; he wasn't mad.

Charlie nodded awkwardly, that was what she had seen, "It was terrible, Kabir. I saw the same thing. I saw it too." she said quietly.

Kabir looked relieved. His eyes filled with tears. He dabbed at them and grabbed his glass of wine and drank deeply. Feeling awkward in the moment.

What was more terrible was that they knew things in that moment. Things that made what they had seen all the more terrible. The animals had been sacrificed and whoever had done it had kept them alive for as long as possible as he cut them open and dissected them. That he enjoyed it and so did the Bad Man. Worse still, the Bad Man needed those sacrifices. He fed on them.

Charlie watched Kabir, not knowing what to do or to say. Knowing that there was precious little she could do. That the space between them was too much and that waiting twenty years to talk about that day had made it even more difficult to come back together and rebuild the friendship that they had let slip away.

She felt one of the photos in her hand, looked down at it. She didn't recognise the place that had been photo'd, it was a country road. Archie would have recognised it instantly, she knew that much. She turned the photo in her fingers to look at the back.

Another short message in the same childish hand writing. A writing style that creeped her out all by itself. She knew that the writer was not a child. That if the writer was at all childish, he or she was the worst of childhood. Cruel. Cruel the way only a child can be.

She read the message again. Her feeling of fear heightened. This one message was a hammer blow and made the threat of whatever was undoubtedly coming for them, very real.

YOU LEFT THE GATE OPEN!

Twenty years ago, they had trespassed. They had gone somewhere that they should not have gone and worse still, they had opened that damned gate. They had pulled that bolt back and they had left it that way.

They had left the gate open.

Even at the time, Charlie had known that was important. That what they had done was wrong. Somehow they had released something out into the world. Something truly bad. Something evil.

The Bad Man.

She didn't know why it was coming for them after this last twenty years. Didn't want to think about what it had been doing during that interval of time. She hoped that it had done nothing but wait. She knew it was ancient and twenty years was nothing to it. That in some ways, they had been gifted the last twenty years.

Now though? There was going to be a reckoning. They couldn't go back. It was too late to close that damn gate. Right now, as Charlie looked at the card, she stared beyond it, back along The Pipe to twenty years ago, she thought that all they could do was choose. They could run and pretend that they stood a chance in running, or they could make a stand and face this thing.

That was the choice they were presented with and she already knew what choice she was going to make.

8

Kabir and Charlie had cleared the macabre photos away and placed them carefully, almost reverentially back in the chocolate tin. Once this was done, it seemed to relieve the oppressive atmosphere that had filled the room and weighed down upon the both of them. They talked about the last twenty years and drank Archie's wine. At some point they realised they were hungry and found a leaflet for pizza place that would deliver.

The house was big and there was plenty of room for both of them. They eventually turned in in the early hours of the morning. Wondering where the time had gone, both today and since they'd been ten years old. Buzzing from the conversation, happy to have caught up, even happier thanks to the wine that had flowed freely. There were several empty bottles on the coffee table and neither of them remembered retrieving and opening the last of them.

Even in the unfamiliar beds and strange circumstances, they slept soundly and they slept until late morning.

Charlie was the first to rise. Surprised and pleased at her ten o'clock lie in, she gave way to a gentle grumble about her contrary sleeping patterns – did it take death and the threat of more death for her to sleep soundly? She took most of her grumble back as she realised that she seemed to be largely hangover free and refreshed despite the lake of wine she'd shared with Kabir.

Soon, she was in the kitchen looking to see what there was by way of provisions. She glanced at the two pizza boxes on the side as she walked in, wondering whether breakfast would be cold left over pizza slices washed down with tap water. It was something and that was always better than nothing. Even better if there were sauces available to add to the pizza. Preferably salad cream, Charlie could make do with pizza and salad cream alright.

She was happy to find fresh milk in the fridge and fresh bread in the bread bin. Kabir had obviously bought a few provisions before Charlie had arrived. She found tea bags and mugs and set about making a brew and toast. There was marg in the fridge. Margarine always seemed to have an inordinately long date on it, a friend once told her that marg was mostly made of the same ingredients as her car tyres, she thought this an exaggeration, but there was a jangling bell of truth to it, marg was manufactured after all. She even found an unopened jar of strawberry jam. Kabir had thought of everything!

Charlie was leaning against the kitchen unit's side eating her second slice of toast and drinking a strong mug of tea when she heard Kabir coming down the stairs. Testament to the size and sturdiness of Archie's place was that this was the first she'd heard of Kabir's surfacings, in her own house she'd have heard everything from the moment Kabir rolled over in bed. She reboiled the kettle and had time to pour the hot water on the teabag before he arrived in the doorway. She was at the fridge as she heard him. She closed the door and saw him standing in the doorway.

"What's up?" she asked.

Charlie had felt upbeat and was all set to greet Kabir in a cheery manner. This dissipated as she saw the look on his face. He looked distraught, almost broken.

Kabir lifted a hand. In it was one of the polaroids.

Charlie's brow knotted – why was he showing her one of Archie's polaroids. Had he thought of something else that he wanted to show her. She put the milk down on the side and stepped over towards him. As she did, she saw that this photo was different. She had not seen this photo before now.

This photo was all wrong. It was sick.

"Fuck," Charlie breathed the word out as she saw the photo for the first time, "where was it?" she asked quietly. Kabir was still holding it out towards her, as though offering it to her. Wanting her to take it from him and relieve him of the burden. She left it there, not wanting to touch it.

"It was on the door mat," he said, equally quietly.

"What does it say?"

"See for yourself," Kabir jerked his arm, jabbing the photo towards Charlie.

She took it grudgingly. Looked once again at the photo on the front of the card, before flipping it to read what was written on the other side.

Again, the same, child-like writing.

It was addressed to this house, the address matching all of the photos in the tin.

The addressees though. That detail differed.

Charlie n Kabir

Again, no stamp and no postmark. Whoever had delivered this had known they were here. Both of them. At Archie's house.

Charlie tried to supress a shudder. Failed. Her mouth was working up and down like a landed trout. Words she wanted to say could not file out towards her mouth as a log jam was forming. Her mind was racing. Some twisted fuck was watching them and he'd...

The message. She read the message.

Your friend is with my master now.

Reading the message and relating it to the photo was too much. The polaroid and it's message made a terrible sense now. It hit Charlie in a powerful and disorienting wave. Something rose up in Charlie and her sight failed her. Her head swam and the floor shifted beneath her. Two strong hands were guiding her. She felt the kitchen sink in front of her. Retched. Leaning forwards and puking. Her body convulsing and purging itself. A spontaneous reset.

She stayed like that for a while. Eyes firmly shut. Unable to open them. Incapable of functioning. She had shut down and her senses were still closed off. It took a while before she felt the kitchen sink again, let alone the reassuring hand stroking her back. Eventually Kabir's voice found a way in.

"It's OK," he repeated softly.

Only it wasn't. It was far from OK. She'd heard the voice as she read the message. She'd heard two voices. The person who had done this to Archie and the Bad Man. She'd heard them in her mind as she'd read the message and then she was there. In The Pipe. Facing all of that carnage. The misery, the suffering and the death. She'd felt the Bad Man behind her. Felt his cold, unyielding hands on the sides of her head as he made her look at his handiwork. Made her look at Archie for the first time in twenty years. Only this was not Archie. Not anymore. It was an abomination.

They had taken Archie's body.

Charlie somehow knew that this was not the Bad Man's usual work. He had rushed it. It was careless and forced. The Bad Man had been unable to do it the way he had wanted to.

And he had really wanted this.

He had waited for so long.

Then this…

DISAPPOINTMENT!

She felt the rage. Intense rage.

The only saving grace was that Archie was dead when the Bad Man had done this to him.

Kabir would not be so lucky.

Charlie certainly would not be so lucky.

He was saving her until last.

As Charlie opened her eyes she understood something else.

Archie's killer had somehow fucked up. Archie had died a merciful death before the Bad Man could do his worst. The Bad Man had been cheated and the Bad Man was now angry and he was still hungry. He was coming for them.

The Bad Man was coming for them.

Charlie composed herself. Washing her face and mouth in the kitchen sink. Glad that Kabir had had the presence of mind to guide her to the sink before she had vomited.

"Thanks Kabir," she forced a smile as she turned away from the sink towards him. She looked at him quizzically, "I didn't know you had this in you…"

"What?" Kabir looked slightly embarrassed as he smirked at her, "being caring? I had younger brothers, remember?"

THE PIPE

Charlie nodded and gave him a knowing look.

"Oh no! You're not doing that!" protested Kabir.

"Doing what?"

"Jumping to the conclusion that I'm gay because I rubbed your back while you were sick!"

Charlie laughed despite herself, "Just remember that you said that. I didn't."

Kabir harumphed at her. Choosing not to say anything more. That was fine by her. They hadn't talked about anyone currently significant in their lives. Both single and in no rush to change that status. They hadn't disclosed anything further. Not their romantic past, nor what it was that might turn their eye, either for a night of distraction or something longer term. It hadn't seemed important and maybe that said something about all three of them. None of them had a significant other. None of them seemed to have had a significant ex. They'd all of them kept themselves to themselves. Withdrawn from the world as though waiting for something to happen, putting their lives of a semi-pause ever since their adventure twenty years ago.

And now something was happening.

Kabir knelt to pick up the photo, "this is for real isn't it?" he said waving it to and fro as though drying it fresh out of the camera.

"I think so," agreed Charlie. "But I think we should do a drive by of the cemetery, once you've had your tea and toast."

Kabir screwed his face up, "I'm not all that hungry, if I'm honest."

"Sorry," shrugged Charlie.

"It's fine, shall we grab our stuff and go?"

Charlie nodded towards the front door, "I'm ready to go when you are." Her bag, a simple rucksack, was packed and by the front door.

Kabir looked a bit confused and upset at this development. This made Charlie feel a little guilty. She'd been ready to go. There was nothing here for her and the sooner she got back home the better. She'd not really thought about what she was doing, it was automatic. Pack up. Get ready. Go home.

She pulled her car keys out of her pocket and held them between herself and Kabir, a distraction and a peace offering both "shall I drive?"

Kabir seemed placated by this. It meant they would spend time together in the car and they would at least return here before departing. Charlie was no longer cutting and running. Not yet anyway.

He left the kitchen to grab his coat from the hallway, Charlie followed, opening the front door. As she did, she found that she was looking at the place on the floor inside the doorway that the polaroid had likely landed. Then she was looking out of the front door and scanning around for something, anything that betrayed the presence of whoever had delivered the polaroid and its message. The deliverer of this dark message had been here only moments ago. And yet neither she nor Kabir had run to the door to try to try to catch them. It were as though they knew there was no point, whoever had delivered the message was long gone, if they had been here at all.

Kabir darted back, deeper into the house and returned holding a piece of pizza in his hand.

"I thought you weren't hungry?" smiled Charlie.

"Changed my mind," Kabir took a bite as he passed her and stepped out onto the gravel drive.

Kabir finished the slice as Charlie drove.

"How was it?" Charlie asked as Kabir burped and hit his chest with his fist as though to dislodge something.

"Magnificent!" said Kabir, "I didn't know how hungry I was until I started eating it!"

They drove along in silence for a while longer. Charlie had made the conscious decision to turn the radio down so it was no longer audible, she thought that filling the car's enclosed space with her noise was rude. More so when she was with a friend she hadn't seen for twenty years and in the context of her faux pas with her packed bag by the door. That had been tactless. They had run twenty years ago and that had been a mistake. It seemed Charlie's default was to run away from trouble. She didn't have to think this one through, she couldn't deny this about herself. She'd been running all her life.

Kabir spoke into the silence, "how are we going to tell whether the coffin is empty?"

Charlie had wondered about this also. The polaroid that they had received

THE PIPE

today was a photo of an empty coffin lying next to an open grave. They were meant to believe that this was Archie's coffin. That the Bad Man and his twisted side kick had taken Archie's body.

"I mean we can't just dig Archie up, can we?"

Charlie turned to look at Kabir, there was serious intent conveyed in her look.

"You can't be serious!" Kabir almost screeched.

When Charlie didn't say anything he muttered inaudibly to himself. He was giving voice to an inner dialogue, then, "No! We can't! We're not Harke and Burr!"

"Who?"

"They're... I read comics OK? It's a play on Burke and Hare. Body snatchers. Only the real guys had a head for business and realised fresh corpses would sell for more and it was easier to kill people than it was to wait around then dig them up..."

"You're rambling," Charlie gently cajoled as she made a right turn.

"Is it any wonder!" Kabir sighed, "have you stopped to think about what we're doing?"

"Yup," said Charlie in response. As driver she didn't see that it was useful to engage in too much conversation. She wanted to concentrate on the road ahead and get them there in one piece. They could think about what they were going to do once they were there.

Kabir made a frustrated keening noise.

"Look, we're not going to dig Archie up, OK?" said Charlie firmly.

"Good!" Kabir wondered why Charlie couldn't have said this in the first place.

"Not in broad daylight, anyway," Charlie tried to supress a smile as she said this. Couldn't help but smile as she was rewarded with another keening noise.

There was quiet again in the car. Although Charlie could almost hear the cogs in Kabir's mind whirring. Eventually the inevitable happened. Kabir spoke just as Charlie was about to turn into the road prior to the one that the cemetery was on.

"Ground penetrating radar!" he exclaimed.

"Now that sounds like a great idea," said Charlie. And it was, except… "Only, will it see through a coffin? Won't it just tell us that there's a coffin there?"

"But they use it to find bodies!" protested Kabir.

"Bodies that are not in coffins…" Charlie dropped that one in. She knew the remains of the murdered had been found by ground penetrating radar. She'd read about it in enough news articles.

"No, archaeologists use it to find properly buried remains!" said Kabir triumphantly!

"Properly buried remains?"

"Yeah, in coffins and shit!" Kabir was excited now. He'd cracked it. No need to dig Archie up.

"And where do we get a ground penetrating radar from? Argos?" said Charlie, blowing a hole in Kabir's idea, right below the plimsol line.

"You sound like my Mum," Kabir said sulkily.

"No need for that Kabir," replied Charlie.

"Sorry, but…" began Kabir.

"No Kabir," Charlie cut across him, "Look!"

Kabir had not been paying attention to anything other than his plan. If he had, then he would have seen the police cars and van. The tape. And, thanks to the raised ground the other side of the cemetery wall, they could see a mound of fresh earth.

"Fuck!" exhaled Kabir.

"Fuck indeed," agreed Charlie.

She was slowing the car.

"What are you doing!?" Kabir was animated. Panicking.

"Parking," said Charlie matter-of-factly.

"Are you mad!?" squealed Kabir.

"No. Now calm down and come with me." Charlie was taking her seatbelt off. She looked across at her friend. And he was her friend. The years had rolled away and they were just the same really. Remarkable how very little had changed and they'd slipped into their old roles. Their usual selves. Kabir was excitable. Charlie was the calmer of the two. It wasn't as simple as that of course, there were a whole host of roles to play, but when you stripped it back it largely became a case of following the same old patterns. Treading well-worn paths. They'd fallen back into it so readily and easily, even in these odd circumstances.

Right now, Kabir was bouncing in the passenger seat.

"Or you can stay here," Charlie added before exiting the car.

"Fuck!" whispered Kabir as he undid his own seatbelt and followed her.

Charlie smiled slightly as Kabir caught up with her. Knew that he would.

There was tape across the entrance to the cemetery. A police constable was standing sentry behind the tape. She saw them approaching and eyed them warily, no doubt having seen more than her fair share of rubber neckers and the terminally and annoyingly nosey. Charlie was surprised that there was not at least a few onlookers already gathered nearby. She looked beyond the tape and saw the usual site to be seen in cemeteries far and wide. Scattered across the cemetery were elderly relatives going about their business and tending to the graves of loved ones. Many were having a conversation with their deceased loved one about the palaver across the way. There was obviously another entrance to the graveyard and none of the interlopers had been a nuisance, so they'd been left to it.

"Sorry, no one is to enter the graveyard," the constable warned as Charlie walked right up to the tape.

Charlie nodded beyond the constable, saw her tense, ready to rebuff a comment about the people already beyond her line, "that's our friend's grave," she explained.

This wrongfooted the constable, "Your friend?"

"Yes, we... attended his funeral yesterday," she had been about to say that they had buried him yesterday. That was what people said wasn't it? Only they hadn't been the ones who had buried him and they certainly hadn't been the ones who had dug him up.

"You were at the funeral yesterday?" asked the constable.

Charlie nodded, "both of us."

The constable made a decision. Charlie liked her for that. This set her apart from the majority of gatekeepers who's only decision was to decide that it was not for them to make any decisions. She lifted the tape, "OK, go and see DS Manners. I'm sure he'll be able to help."

Kabir peered past her, "Manners?"

The constable nodded, "You'll know which one he is," she said, a smirk playing across her lips.

Manners was the red faced man shouting at everyone else. He stood in the midst of the team and didn't seem happy about anything, least of all being there.

"I thought I told..." he began to bark at Charlie.

"We were here for Archie's funeral yesterday," said Charlie calmly. She didn't mention the constable. Didn't want her involved, she'd done her bit.

"You..." Manners began and then saw that both Charlie and Kabir were staring at the open coffin. It lay at an angle, an end partially hanging over the hastily dug six foot hole. Hastily dug as although there was one main pile of earth, there were also clods of earth around and about. The digging had been frantic and messy. This gave the impression of the coffin having been discarded. It looked like a strange piece of litter. An empty container discarded once whatever was inside had been consumed.

"I'm sorry," Manners changed tack entirely as he saw how shocked both Charlie and Kabir looked, "you shouldn't have had to see this."

He walked towards them, collected them and sat them away from the scene on one of the many benches to be found in the cemetery. He gently asked them questions and quickly established that they knew nothing useful or helpful to him and his investigation. He handed them cards, just in case.

For their part, Kabir and Charlie said very little. There was nothing for them to say. They had got what they had come for. They had seen it with their own eyes. And in seeing the open coffin and the absence of their friend's body it was now, all too real. Not that it hadn't been real before now. This discovery removed any chance for them to go into denial and pretend the polaroids were a prank by a twisted, but ultimately harmless fuck.

Seeing Archie's open coffin, and the absence of his body left them in no doubt.

THE PIPE

They were fucked.
The Bad Man was coming for them.

9

Charlie had needed to get away from there. She felt the pull of home more than ever now. In any case, she needed to get back for Shap. She knew she was running, but she had to have some time out. Go to her safe place and think things through. Work out what to do from the safety of her sanctuary.

Kabir had been disappointed. He didn't want her to go. And he didn't want to go home. He'd asked about Archie's place and the will and a number of details that they needed to get sorted. She explained that in this day and age, they could do that from their respective homes.

Kabir had not been placated and he hadn't let her leave without a promise that they would see each other again soon. She had agreed and she had meant it. It had been great to see Kabir again and there was the pressing matter of those polaroids and the person behind the threats written on each and every one of them.

He'd begun some half formed words about the police and The Pipe and it was evident that he hadn't thought it through and perhaps didn't want to think it through, but then he had blurted something out.

"We need to go back to The Pipe."

He'd said it as a statement and once it was out there they knew he was right. They had to go back.

They were equally shocked by his words. Neither of them had ever wanted to go near that place again. Knew that they should never gone there in the first place, and yet there was a pull towards The Pipe. Always had been. It had haunted them ever since that day twenty years ago. Now Kabir had voiced the one thing they had both been trying to avoid. Knowing that once the words were said. Once their darkest desire had been said out loud. They would return.

They knew that they had to.

Eventually, Charlie had nodded. The nod was not to say that she would go right there and then, nor was it a yes, that she would definitely go. All she was doing was to acknowledge what Kabir had said and for now that was enough. She couldn't stomach anymore right now.

"I have to go Kabir," Charlie had said, "but I hear you. I'll call when I get back. I need to regroup and have space and time to think. This is a lot to take in."

Kabir had nodded gravely, "just don't leave it too long, OK?" He was the next on the list and very conscious that he had limited time before this thing caught up with him.

"Where will you be?" asked Charlie.

"I might stick around here for a while." Kabir had left things open ended. He'd known about the will and given himself time to look at what was needed and do as much as he could while he stayed at Archie's house.

He'd wanted to avoid his flat in the hope that he wouldn't see any more of those damn polaroids, but Archie's tin box and the arrival of the polaroid of the open coffin had put paid to that. He'd smiled and told Charlie he might stay at Archie's to make life difficult for the Polaroid Man. Kabir wasn't all that familiar with the area, so it would make it more difficult to photograph places and things familiar to him. The smile had not been all that convincing. Just talking about the prospect of receiving more photos and the short messages on the other side of them was too much. What had seemed a strange and twisted joke had turned into something much more terrible and neither of them could quite believe it. They both wanted to discover that it was a prank made in bad taste. Archie's last acts before he died. Ill judged, but once the dust had settled strangely poignant. A last piece of a friend they should never have lost touch with. If only they had never discovered The Pipe. Things would have been different then. Better.

As Charlie was leaving, she turned back to her friend, a detail of that fateful day had just occurred to her, "Kabir?"

"Yes?" he smiled hopefully at her from the open doorway.

"If we go back, promise me one thing?"

"Yes?" he was intrigued now.

"You'll bring more than one torch."

She'd grinned at him and he'd laughed. That had been good, that they could still laugh despite everything. It was the right note to part on.

Charlie watched Kabir in her rear view mirror as she drove away. He waved until they lost sight of each other. He looked diminished, small and dejected. She felt like she was deserting him, which in a way, she was.

She turned her music up, switching from the radio to a CD. Her car was an old model and CDs were the best it could do. She didn't mind, enjoyed listening to albums.

Charlie did some of her best thinking when she drove. It was a variation on dreaming. Her mind free formed and as it did so, things would fall into place and make a certain kind of sense. It was sometimes frustrating as she couldn't write anything down and her train of thought could all too easily be obliterated by an inconsiderate driver. Once a train of thought was gone, just like a dream, there was no way to find it and start up where you had left off.

Kabir had mumbled something about the police. That they should go to the police. It was an obvious port of call and one that Charlie had also leapt at, but she didn't think for one moment that it would play out the way they would want it to. They'd seen the police at Archie's graveside. Charlie could imagine how it would go if they tried to explain that their childhood bogeyman was stalking them. Sending them photos with notes scribbled on the back. DS Manners didn't look like the open minded sort and an ill thought out approach could well implicate them in the disappearance of Archie's body and perhaps something much worse.

Anything they said would not make sense to anyone else. They would appear mad and Charlie didn't fancy a long stay in a secure unit where any protestation of her innocence and explanation of her perfectly normal sanity would earn her an even longer stay in her very own bedroom, complete with a set of crayons and meals of mashed banana.

Charlie had worried about her sanity ever since Billy had died. She'd seen her parents fall apart and her Dad's mental health had been the death of him. Her Mum had lived, but the quality of her life wasn't much better than her Dad's fate. Charlie was the daughter of two people who's mental health had deteriorated and these things could be hereditary couldn't they? That was another reason for her to stay under the radar and avoid the police and the professionals they called upon to deal with people and process people like Charlie.

Besides, they didn't have all that much time and she didn't want to waste it with the police.

This was their battle and Charlie thought that it would only make matters worse if they tried to involve anyone else. At the very least, roping someone else in would put that person in danger and not help Charlie or Kabir one bit. Charlie didn't want to make matters worse. This was all her fault and she had to do something about it.

This left Charlie and Kabir alone and with the prospect of a return to The Pipe.

They were older now. Bigger. Bolder. Charlie latched onto her experiences of returning to childhood places. Remembered a visit to a primary school and the tiny seats that she struggled to imagine ever sitting on. Surely she had never been that small? The size of those seats had made the school seem farcical and alien to her.

She hoped The Pipe had changed that way too, that if would be smaller and less daunting. That should they return to their old stomping grounds their fears and concerns would evaporate and they would be left feeling foolish. Perhaps then everything would go away. And if it didn't they could go to the police about their odd stalker in the hope that a visit from the police would put the weirdo off.

Only, where would the police go and what would they do? They didn't know who was doing this? And whoever it was was twisted enough to steal Archie's body. They had followed Charlie and Kabir and known that they were at Archie's house.

9

Then there was The Pipe itself.

Charlie found herself thinking about Kabir's description of what he'd seen. A carefully organised array of defiled bodies. Piled high, but in a way that meant something. Someone had butchered creatures alive and done it again and again and again over a protracted period. They were sacrifices to the Bad Man. Now this twisted fucker was stalking them. Had taken their friend's body and was promising them the same fate as those animals. Archie had been the lucky one. The Bad Man would not let Kabir or Charlie cheat him of his prey. Of his sacrifice. Of his meal.

They had to go back to The Pipe. That was where this had all started. That was where there would be answers. That's where they would stop this thing.

Charlie found herself on the home stretch, the drive home had gone by in a blur. Kabir had texted soon after she left, probably as he went back into Archie's house.

Safe journey. Drop me a line when you get back

She read it as she walked to her front door. If they had been dating, she'd seriously consider ignoring him with a view to cooling things off and dumping him. Unless of course she was smitten, in which case this sort of attentiveness would be exactly what she wanted. As it was, he was a concerned friend and he was a friend in need. She wouldn't walk away this time. She couldn't.

She struggled to get the door open, rucksack slipping off her shoulder, phone and keys in the same hand, fighting not to drop them. The key turned in the lock after a couple of failed attempts. The door swung open and Charlie gasped. There on the mat was another of the polaroids.

She hadn't expected it. Not now. Not so soon.

If she was honest with herself, she'd thought that it was Kabir's turn first and that she would be spared this. At least for a while. She'd thought that she had more time.

Numb. Not wanting to believe the evidence of her eyes. There, but not present. Shap barking. Drawing her back in. Needing her. She stepped over the photo and into the house. Kicking the door closed. Dumping her bag at the foot of the stairs. Going in to see Shap. So excited to see her. Jumping up towards her, but careful not to catch her with his feet. Not calming for a while so she had to wait. Reaching out a hand to catch him briefly as he jumped up and down, up and down. Waiting. Then crouching down and letting herself be bowled over by his exuberance. His wet nose snuffling at her and his tongue in her ear.

Shap had missed her.

She made a cup of tea. Trying to ignore the photo on the doormat. Knowing what it was. Knew what it was before she had ever seen it.

Billy.

It was never an accident. Billy was the next step. Moving on from the animals and breaking another taboo. That had gone wrong too. But whoever was doing this had learnt. They would not stop and they would carry on perfecting what they saw as their art. Their calling.

Tea half drunk and forgotten, she marched back to her front door. *Her* front door, you fuck! This bastard was violating her space. He'd killed her brother. He'd killed Billy. He'd…

She had the piece of card in her hand. Slid down the wall as she looked at it. Unaware that she was crying. Blinking away the tears so she could see the photo of Billy laying there in the forest. Looking for all the world like he had fallen into a deep sleep.

She turned the card over. The same childlike writing, but this was no child. Maybe he had been when he had killed Billy, but if so, he was a man now. A twisted murderer.

The message…

He was my first!

You made me do it!

You shouldn't have gone into My Pipe!

Charlie threw back her head and screamed.

10

"You called," Kabir sounded genuinely pleased.

"Did you ever doubt it?" Charlie's voice was dull and monotone.

Kabir paused, had wanted to say that yes, he had doubted it. He had put his money on Charlie opting for radio silence, there had after all been twenty years of that, but he thought the smarter money was on the compromise of a few half-hearted texts that took longer and longer to arrive eventually fading back into nothing.

For Kabir's part, he knew that it really could end with *and then nothing*. So he wasn't just pleased, he was relieved. In this endeavour, Charlie was his only friend. The only person who would understand. And she had called him the day after going home. He'd worried when she hadn't replied to his text. He wasn't a worrier in normal circumstances. Generally he assumed that no news was good news. But these were not normal circumstances. Someone was out there and whoever he was, he was far from normal. He was so far from normal, normal didn't get a look in.

Charlie had called, but she did not sound right. She sounded far from alright. She sounded dead inside.

"Charlie... what's happened?" asked Kabir. He could hear her laboured breathing. It sounded like the aftermath of sobbing to him.

Charlie was sat on the sofa with Shap. He had his head on her lap and was staring up at her. She was stroking him. He was helping. Without Shap she probably would have fallen apart completely. Wouldn't have been able to have made this call.

"Did you get another photo, Kabir?" she asked in the same monotone.

Kabir had. He had it in front of him as they spoke, "Yes, it was there waiting for me this morning."

There was something in his voice. There was more to this than Kabir was saying, "Where was the photo, Kabir?"

"Charlie, why are you asking me that?" Charlie asking the sixty four million dollar question had caught Kabir out. How did she know to ask that question?

"It's your voice. The photo wasn't simply dropped through the letter box was it?"

"No," Kabir let out a long, low breath, "it was on my car and I suppose you could say that it was inside a cat…"

"Shit…" Charlie immediately knew what Kabir meant. Really wished that she didn't. Their stalker had opened up a cat and used it to package Kabir's next photo. She looked down at Shap and shuddered unexpectedly at the thought of what this mad man might do. "Show me," Charlie demanded.

"Charlie it's…" Kabir began.

"You took a photo didn't you?" Charlie knew he must have. It was what she would have done. It's what anyone else would have done. People took photos automatically now. It was the way that you recorded your life. A picture spoke a thousand words and people took thousands of photos. They captured memories and stories in an instant.

"I did," confirmed Kabir, "but you don't…"

"Kabir, we're in this together. We need to do something about this fucking prick, so just send me the bloody photo, OK!"

Charlie's phone went dead. Kabir had ended the call. She raised an eyebrow, he could have sent the photo whilst on the call. She censured herself, Kabir would know that. He'd chosen to end the call.

Her phone pinged. She had a new message. She opened her messages, another pinged up. A second message from Kabir.

The first message was the photo of the cat. It had been cut from neck to crotch and opened up wide. The cavity had been emptied of its innards and the photo was placed in the centre. Kabir had added a few words to the picture.

So he's taken to framing his photos!

10

The second message was also from Kabir.
I recognised the photo – it's the end of Archie's road.
The message on the other side is brutal…
I'm going to open you up like this fucking cat and you'll be alive and awake through it all! And that's just for starters lol!
Charlie's phone rang. It was Kabir.
"Fucked up isn't it?"
"You don't know the half of it," Charlie said quietly.
"Why? What's happened?" asked Kabir.
"I had a photo waiting for me when I got back."
"Shit," said Kabir. He could tell it was bad. His mind was racing as he tried to second guess what this sick fuck had sent to Charlie.
"He killed Billy…" Charlie's voice cracked and she stifled a sob.
Kabir expelled a long breath. Almost groaned with the weight of what he had heard.
"Do you know what the worst of it is? I knew. I always knew that what happened to Billy was because of me."
Hearing talk like that was terrible. Kabir could feel her hurt and worse than that, she was broken by it, "Don't talk like that Charlie, it was never your fault."
"It was! We should never have gone into that fucking pipe!"
"We were kids! How were we to know!?"
"Oh we knew alright. We sensed how bad that place was and still we went in! How stupid and arrogant were we, Kabir?! Worse still, we left that gate unlocked. We let him out!!"
"No, Charlie. We did not. He's using us as an excuse for what he does. You saw what was in that pipe. He was killing well before we ever turned up. He must have seen us and taken that photo. Now he's blaming us for what he does. But it's not our fault. He would have killed regardless."
"He wouldn't have killed Billy, Kabir," Charlie retorted.
"You don't know that. He probably didn't even know who Billy was. Wrong kid in the wrong place."
Charlie sighed, another sob threatening to break into a torrent of tears, "I

knew that place was dangerous and I ignored the danger. After we went in there, I ran away and pretended it was going to be OK, and it never was was it?"

"We couldn't have known, Charlie. Like we couldn't have known this was going to happen all these years later."

"Because of me, Billy is dead. And then my Dad killed himself."

"Charlie, don't do this," Kabir was pleading with her now, "this is exactly what he wants. He's taunting us and he's playing us. He wants to frighten the crap out of us and put us on the back foot. We can't let him win!"

"He won twenty years ago, Kabir. We just didn't know it."

Kabir shook his head at his phone, "Don't quit on me, Charlie! We can't let him win. We have to stop him. We have to at least try don't we?"

Kabir heard Charlie sigh again, "Yes."

One word, but it was the right word. It was enough.

Kabir went on, moving the subject on slightly, "how's he getting these photos delivered?"

"I'm only two hours away, Kabir. And my photo was waiting for me here. He had a couple of days didn't he?"

"I suppose so, but the photos. Everything about them. They freak me out. That first one. We all got the same one. That's not possible. Taken from an angle that must've been in The Pipe, but couldn't have been. I mean there was no one in The Pipe when we went in was there, and even if there was, he would have needed a flash and we'd have seen it wouldn't we? It's not faded like photos do over the years. And he's hand delivering them. Don't even get me started on the freaky writing either."

"OK, we're agreed on the photos being freaky and totally fucked up." Charlie sounded a little more upbeat. More alive. This was reassuring. Kabir needed Charlie in the room. Charlie needed Charlie in the room.

"And we're agreed that this is something to do with The Pipe." Kabir left that there. He didn't know how long they had, more importantly he didn't know how long he had. What he did know was that they needed to go back. The Pipe was important and there may be answers there. It felt like taking the fight to this freak if they went to The Pipe. It was better than waiting for him to come for them. And he was coming. The dead cat and the photo of Billy left them in no doubt about that. He was watching them, playing with them and he was serious. Deadly serious.

"You want to go to The Pipe don't you, Kabir? Have you not thought that that's exactly what he wants? Wouldn't we be doing that thing in films where people go into the basement when what they should do is get the hell out of the house?"

"It doesn't feel like that, Charlie," Kabir said matter-of-factly, "what's the alternative?"

Charlie had thought about this. She'd had plenty of time to think. Sleep had eluded her last night, so all she could do as she lay there in her bed was think about the past and what all of this meant and what she might do about it.

"There isn't one," she said, knowing that there was. They both knew that the obvious option was to run. To get away and hope whoever was behind this would not find them. He would though. He would find them wherever they went.

He had waited twenty years.

And now he was coming for them.

11

They had agreed that Charlie would come back via Archie's place and then Kabir would drive them both back to their childhood home town.

There were arrangements to be made. The practicalities of life. Charlie needed to square things with her boss, and as it turned out, her boss was amenable to her taking time off at short notice, but she *was* needed for the rest of the week before she could take that time off.

Then there was Shap, the neighbours were great when it was a day or two here or there, but this may take longer. She'd agreed with Kabir that they would need to take at least two weeks. They had no idea what they were going to do once they got there, nor how long it would take. As it was, Laura her neighbour three doors down from her, was all too keen to have Shap for the whole duration. Her kids were mithering her for a dog and she wanted to see how they would live up to their promised responsibilities. Would they really walk the dog twice a day? Pick up after it? Wash it and groom it? Or would they swiftly tire of the hard work and leave it all to Mum?

Charlie didn't want to tell her that what was most likely was the kids would make the effort for the whole two weeks and repeat that effort to begin with with their own dog. If there was going to be any trouble, it would start a few months in, and then Laura would be lumbered. Not that it was a problem. The small amount of effort required to look after a dog was paid back tenfold by the dog, and then some.

Even before the mooted two week break, Kabir had already done his ground work. He could work remotely and all he had to worry about was someone watering his single and solitary plant, the one living thing in his flat, if you didn't count the mould that occasionally sprouted up in his bachelor fridge. He joked that as it was a cactus, even that wasn't a problem. He said he would use the rest of the week to look further into the will and what this meant for them both. One way or another, he'd told Charlie, he'd keep himself busy. She was sure that he would.

As it was, Charlie struggled at work. She wasn't sleeping. It wasn't just the revelation that the Bad Man had got Billy that had got her mind racing with a myriad of what ifs. There was Archie and Kabir and the photos. Everything went back to their home town and everything went back down The Pipe.

And that was it. The focal point. The Pipe and the Bad Man were inextricably linked. She felt that and she felt their presence now in the same way that she had on that fateful day and for every day that she had remained in her home town of Dinsdale. Then she had moved away and although The Pipe never left her dreams she had moved on. She had moved on until that polaroid appeared of the three of them at The Pipe all those years ago.

Why now? Why after all these years was this happening? Surely the Bad Man hadn't lain dormant for twenty years, then woken up with revenge on his mind. Revenge for them having trespassed?

It was Thursday night, she was dog tired and didn't know how she could still be awake, but when sleep hadn't come, she had sat in her bed looking at her tablet. Searching. Typing in the word Dinsdale. A word she had done her best to forget, never using it, trying her best never to think about it. Now she was typing the word and looking for other suspicious deaths in the area. There were none. Her search found articles on Billy's death and that was a knife in her heart. There were also accounts of her father's death on the anniversary of his son's death. A tragedy that he had been unable to come to terms with and that had ultimately taken his life also. After that there was nothing of note that Charlie could find. There were a couple of car accidents resulting in deaths. Teenagers going too fast and misjudging the local roads. A motorcyclist colliding with a tree.

Charlie could not find anything related to Dinsdale Woods or the surrounding area. Either the Bad Man had been very good at covering his tracks and Charlie's searches hadn't picked up on a string of missing people, or he'd stopped.

Either that, or he had moved.

Charlie froze. That was possible wasn't it? In the same way that the effect The Pipe had had on her had diminished when she and her mother had moved away. Couldn't this be the reason why whoever was doing this had paused? In her mind's eye she saw an outline image of an older kid. A loner. That was who had seen them on that fateful day and taken a polaroid picture of them. The Pipe was his place, and the three of them had discovered it and made him angry.

If his folks had needed to move away, then he'd have had no choice, he would have had to go with them. Perhaps he had only now returned and that was when they'd picked back up on their old arrangement, him and the Bad Man.

Charlie didn't bother looking at the time on the tablet clock, that held no meaning for her right now. She was too tired and spaced out to appreciate that she had gone into the early hours of Friday morning. She dropped Kabir a series of texts as she thought her theory through. They needed to find a way to discover who had moved away from the area at a similar time that she had. Families with school aged kids. Surely, in this data rich age, there was a way to do this?

Not surprisingly, there was no instant reply from Kabir and something about the discovery of this theory, and the potential breakthrough that it promised must have relaxed Charlie enough for sleep to creep up on her and take her. She'd made a little progress and she had something to focus on. Something to do.

The next thing Charlie knew, was that Shap was on her bed and licking her face. She gently batted him away several times, wanting to cling onto precious and much needed sleep. Barely conscious and not really appreciating what was happening. Shap was persistent though and eventually got his way by licking noisily at her ear. Charlie crawled out from under him and searched for her phone on the bedside table, nearly breaking the screen of the forgotten and discarded tablet as she leant on it with her elbow.

Her eyes remained blurry as she pressed the phone screen into life. The time on the home screen did not register, nor make sense.

10.10

"Shit!" Charlie was suddenly bolt upright and Shap struggled to keep his feet and stay on the duvet as it launched into a tidal wave in reaction to Charlie's sudden movement. The tablet was not so lucky, it was launched into the air and landed screen down on the floor, but somehow stayed in one piece.

Charlie flung herself out of bed and into the bathroom. Shap watched her go, gave forth with a brief and quiet whine, then lay down on the warm patch of the bed to await her return. He jumped and winced a couple of times as toothpaste tubes fell into sinks and aerosols dived onto the tiled floor. There was a cacophony of sound as Charlie rushed at getting ready and as a result took longer than was absolutely necessary.

She ran around the bedroom collecting clothes and putting some of them on in a haphazard manner. Then she was off along the landing and down the stairs.

"Shap!" she called back up the stairs.

Shap did not come when called. This was all a bit much for him and he'd rather wait it out on the warm bed, thank you. So Charlie was back upstairs and saving time by carrying the mutt back down stairs so she could feed him and let him out. He was heavier than she had bargained for. Neither of them were used to this method of conveyance and both made a mental note not to make a habit of it.

Charlie fed Shap. Or rather, she put food out in front of him. He whined and looked at her sadly before trotting to the back door. He needed the loo and this break with routine really was too much. Charlie let out a howl of frustration. Shap sat and looked at her wondering if he was the reason for her frustration. It shouldn't have been possible, but he managed to look even sadder. He paused at the now open door to make sure Charlie was OK. He nudged her with his nose to see if this helped.

Charlie took one look at Shap's face and dialled it all down a cog. She went outside with him and made a fuss of him.

"You alright old chap?" she asked as she crouched down. He nudged at her gently with his head by way of a response. He was now.

Charlie rang work as Shap was eating, "I'm really sorry! I overslept!"

Her boss was understanding, he'd seen how tired she'd looked over the last week. He even asked whether she was up to coming in. She assured him that she was and ended the call before calling Laura and apologising to her for being late. Laura was fine, said the timing worked even better for her and offered to come over and collect Shap now if that was OK?

It was, and this allowed Charlie time to run upstairs to pack a bag so she could go head to Archie's and Kabir straight from work. She figured this would take some of the pressure off her, heading off straight after work.

The day went by in a blur. Charlie more than made up for her lost time, but the entire day felt like she was catching up. She had wanted to ensure she left work in good shape in any case, so she was a whirlwind of activity and the only reason she came to a stop was it was a Friday and everyone else was heading off. The string of departing colleagues gradually took the wind out of her sales enough that she realised that it was also time for her to leave work and head up to see Kabir.

She could put it off no longer. She put her out of office on, shut her machine down, said goodbye to an empty office and heading out to her car and on to Kabir and then to Dinsdale and The Pipe.

12

The long summer nights can be deceptive. The light barely changes until most of the night is done. There was only a slight darkening around the very edges of the sky as Charlie approached Archie's house. She had had such a full on day that she hadn't stopped and only now did she glance at the clock in her car and note that it was gone nine o'clock of the pm.

She hoped that Kabir wasn't expecting her much before this. As she thought about her expected arrival time, she also thought about her phone. She patted the inside pocket of her jacket and felt the shape of it. She'd not looked at her phone all day. Not since the mad rush this morning when she'd made the call to work flagging her tardiness and the call to Laura to arrange the collection of Shap.

There was a sudden *ping!* Her dashboard lit up with a yellow warning. She had also failed to keep an eye on the instruments in her car and now she was being warned that she was very low on fuel and needed to address this at the earliest possible opportunity.

Charlie suddenly felt anxious. The warning light had given her a jolt and she was now completely knocked out of the full tilt charge she'd made at her day. Work was done and she now had a couple of weeks off, so she could focus completely on this. She now knew that she'd latched onto that total focus and been happy to put her blinkers on. Now though she felt something really bad. The fuel warning light was the messenger. Yes, she really resented the insistent warning and the countdown of the final available miles before she would be stranded. There was something grating and gratuitous about that range countdown and the way the warning light obscured all else including the dashboard clock. It was annoying and raised her stress levels.

Now, as her stress levels were rising, she knew that it wasn't the fuel that was getting to her.

Something was wrong.

Something really was badly wrong.

Charlie felt sick with worry. Things were out of kilter and she'd kidded herself that she was fine and that everything would work out, but right now, events were conspiring against her. She was going to be proven wrong. It was a premonition of sorts. Something was awaiting her and it was bad and it was wrong, so wrong.

The range dropped from 32 miles to 24.

That was another thing that Charlie hated about the range counter, it ran off a logic that was not discernible to her. The warning came in too late in the day and then the promised range was never anywhere near what it should be. Not when it counted down anyway.

The range crept back up to 26 miles and hung there for a while.

Charlie kicked herself. She'd thought that this stretch of her journey was the approach to Archie's house, but she had been premature in thinking this and it were as though she were being punished for her presumption, the fuel light had jumped up in her face as she thought of this as the last stretch.

She was still on the dual carriageway and after this stretch there was more dual carriageway and then the ring road around the nearest large town. She eased off so she was travelling at that supposedly optimum fifty six miles an hour. As though in response to her attempt at maximising the miles she got out of the remaining fuel in the tank, the range jumped again.

26 miles blurred and reappeared as 17 miles.

That was not good. Charlie's car did not have satnav, but she reckoned she was further out from Archie's than the indicated 17 mile fuel tank range. She checked her line of thinking, don't be silly Charlie! She just had to find a petrol station. That was all.

This simple thought should have placated her.

But another thought superseded this, she needed to get to Archie's and she

12

needed to get there right now!

The urgency caused by the warning light and the wayward range counter wasn't about the fuel and the prospect of running out of fuel, it was all about getting to where she needed to be and getting there as quickly as she could. Time was running out. It didn't feel like it was too late right at this moment, it was going to be too late soon though. She needed to hurry. She needed to get there. Her foot crept back down on the accelerator and she gritted her teeth, gripping the steering wheel more tightly as she willed the car on to their destination.

Ahead of her, a sea of red lights. She did not respond at first. Then her brow creased as she realised what it was that she was seeing. A moment later she reacted.

"Shit!" she lifted off the accelerator and had to jam her foot on the brake pedal as her car bore down on the stationary traffic ahead of her. The brake pedal kicked back at her as she ground her foot against it. The rear of the car she was approaching grew ominously as her car came at it too quickly. She stopped her car with barely a foot between the front bumper of her car and the rear bumper of the car in front, so distracted she had been by the need for her to get to Archie's as quickly as she could.

"No!" she shouted at the backs of the cars in front of her. "Shit! Shit! Shit!" she was hitting her steering wheel in frustration at the delay.

She cautioned herself to calm down, bobbing animatedly in her seat she looked around her, hoping to see something. Anything. There were no signs, no pending exits. Nothing. She was stranded and she had nothing.

13 miles.

Her dashboard gloated at her as they sat there in the motionless traffic.

"You can just fuck right off you wanky bastard!" she hissed at the reading on her dash, "you are really not helping matters!"

She sat there for a while, failing to believe her luck. It was nine thirty in the evening. She should have sailed through at this time of night having avoided rush hour. There must be an accident ahead.

Her car was stationary. The traffic was going nowhere. She put the handbrake on and switched the engine off. Watched the car ahead for signs of movement, knowing if it was going to move any time soon, now was the time because she'd only just switched her engine off. That was how stop start motoring usually worked. Nothing. Even tempting providence wasn't going to help this time.

She sighed and resigned herself to sitting here for the foreseeable. Remembered her phone. Lifted it out of her pocket. Nothing. No message notifications. That was strange. She opened her messages anyway. Nothing from Kabir.

Charlie stared at her phone. Nothing from Kabir. She opened the message chain between her and Kabir. Yes, she'd sent her theory to him last night. Well, at three am if she was being more precise about the timing. And there was confirmation that the message had sent.

She considered calling him. Only she couldn't. There was zero signal at this spot on the dual carriageway. She moved her phone around her in the vain hope that she would find a signal. As she moved it to the right she saw a van passing her on the opposite carriageway. It was more a blur of movement that she recognised as van shaped.

Then time stopped. She felt this inexplicable darkness pass over her. Something terrible had happened and this was the very moment that events tipped in the wrong direction. When things went against her.

Charlie was too late.

13

In the scheme of things, a half hour delay to a car journey isn't all that bad. Less so on a Friday evening. The trivial nature of a half hour lost at this time of day is underlined by the measure of lost work hours. Road and rail delays are measured in the hours lost by businesses, not individuals. The only lost time that counts is the time lost in the morning getting everyone to work.

When someone is late, this is viewed in a dim light. The individual in question should have set out earlier and built in a contingency for such a delay. How often was the course of a life changed by the failings of a rail or road network? It was a numbers game though. Most people could soak the delay up. It was no biggy.

The ignominy of Charlie's situation was made all the worse by the fact that once the traffic began moving and she emerged from the stationary crowd of vehicles, there was no clue as to what it was that had caused the delay. If she were to search for a cause for the delay, there would be no record of it. There certainly had been no accident. It was one of those inexplicable delays.

It was the shit that happened.

And it was scant consolation to Charlie that her car eked out the remainder of its fuel and made it to the fuelling station. The CCTV cameras captured the image of Charlie as she filled her car to the brim. She didn't think it through, but she was filling her car so she could drive it to Dinsdale. Her sense of urgency remained, only she was more considered now and it didn't occur to her to partially fill the tank to save precious seconds. This she would consider later, wondering how it was that she knew that she would be driving there in her own car.

Alone.

If you were to zoom in a little and observe Charlie at the garage forecourt, you would see someone who looked done in. World weary. There was no vim and certainly no vigour. Some of the stuffing had been knocked out of her. She already knew she'd lost this round and she would blame herself for her arrogance and her continuing presumption of immortality for the rest of her life.

Charlie was barely thirty and not yet out of that period in her life where death wasn't really a consideration. She could go anywhere and do anything. Thoughts of risk and mortality would come later in her thirties, as it did for most people. She had clung onto that belief that things would be alright. That she had time. Because that was what you did at her stage in life.

Maybe she had had time.

She didn't any longer.

* * *

She drove slowly towards Archie's house, well under the speed limit. It was dark now. Not the proper dark of winter, this dark was a tone of blue. The night never really quite fell during this part of the year, it was already getting lighter before it ever managed to get near full dark. The sun was never all that far away.

As she drove along the street towards Archie's house she could feel it. Even before she could see the façade of Archie's house, she knew. She felt sick as she pulled into the driveway. The house was in darkness. No one was there.

She was too late.

She almost stumbled as she pulled herself out of the car. Her legs were like lead and yet also like jelly as she trembled. At first she wasn't conscious of the words she was whispering over and over.

I'm so sorry Kabir.

13

I'm so sorry Kabir.

She should have been here. She shouldn't have left. Kabir had been a sitting duck. Even in the face of Archie's death and the weird photos they had all received, they had refused to believe anything bad could happen to them. They pretended that it wasn't real. This was not a part of their reality and if they believed hard enough then that belief alone would keep it at bay.

The order they created in their humdrum lives was insubstantial. It was straw that the wolf would cast aside and laugh away as he came for them. And come he had. He had come and he had taken Charlie's friend.

How foolish had Charlie been to think that she had time? That it was important to square things with her boss when her friend's life was at stake?

They said that life went on. Charlie supposed it meant that you had to hold on to the life that you had. That the routine of your day to day would keep you grounded and prevent you from being cast adrift. Sometimes, life got in the way of what was really important.

She walked to the front door, as though in a dream. So convinced had she been that nothing bad could happen to Kabir, not here, not yet anyway, that her entire body was threatening to shut down and go on strike at the unfairness of it all. She wanted to scream, but that would have been an acceptance. That would have made it all the more real and she couldn't afford for it to be. She still had a chance. She might be wrong.

The door was slightly ajar. She stopped in her tracks. There was blood spattered on the outside of the door. She used her foot to push the door inwards. Soundlessly it traced a gentle curve inwards. There was a smear of blood on the hallway floor, it stood out starkly against the black and white tiles.

Then a wave of something foul hit Charlie as she stood in the doorway. A foul stench of death. She gagged and covered her mouth. Her eyes were wide with fear and recognition. A huge knife of ice pierced her as her childhood terror revisited her. This was the smell from The Pipe.

The Bad Man had been here and taken her friend.

Now she was stumbling as she entered the house. She was silent as she walked down the hall. She did not want to be heard, did not want to attract any attention. It was too late for Kabir in any case. Kabir was not here. The Bad Man had taken him. She sensed Kabir's absence. There was no one in this house. She walked down the hall to the kitchen.

The wall unit lights had been left on in this room. This was intentional. Charlie saw this was so as the light illuminated a small object on the work surfaces. Her eye was drawn to it and in the next heart beat she saw what was underneath it. Another of the polaroids.

"Oh god no!" she breathed, slumping against the doorway.

The object on the work surface was a mess. It was partially coated in blood and gore and there were smears of blood on the kitchen work surfaces. Charlie noticed more of the same on the floor. Charlie also noticed something on the floor by the fridge. It was partially under the fridge. She went over to retrieve it, glad of the distraction from the object on the kitchen side and the next polaroid that had been left for her and her alone.

It was Kabir's phone. The screen was smashed. Charlie wasn't going to get any more messages from Kabir.

She turned towards the object on the work surface. She was closer now. It looked like gristle. Something cut from a joint of meat. Her mind raced as she tried to place it. Wondered what it could be. She felt bile in the back of her throat. Whatever it was, it had recently been a piece of Kabir. The Bad Man had cut or torn it from Kabir. Both to torment and play with Kabir before taking him away and to do similar to Charlie. The Bad Man was sending her a message and terrifying her for good measure.

She found that she was edging closer to the work surface. Cautious and reluctant, part of her not wanting to discover what it was that was sitting there waiting for her. Knowing that this was only part of the message. There was a photo and there would be a further message written in that awful, child-like hand. Written by a cruel over grown child who's play things were alive as he took them apart bit by bit.

Charlie was standing at the kitchen side now. Almost over the gristly object itself. She was looking down and from this angle she could see that the meat and gore was only on the side that had been presented to her when she walked in. The rest of the object was round. She couldn't help herself, she reached down and picked the object up. Lifted it and turned it so she could see the other side and the other side saw her.

It was Kabir's eye.

Charlie gagged. She wanted to throw the eye away. Inexplicably, she instead placed it carefully to one side. Wiping her sticky fingers on her jeans feverishly. Rubbing them against the denim material long after they were dry. It would be a while before they felt clean to Charlie.

The Bad Man had taken one of Kabir's eyes.

She lifted the polaroid. Wiped it's surface on the leg of her jeans so she could read the message.

That's just for starters, Charlie!!!
What fun!!! Oh how we laughed!!!
Well I laughed!!! Kabir didn't seem to get the joke!!!
I'm sure he will eventually...
...I'll make sure he does!!!
Come and join us Charlie!!!!!!

Her hand was shaking badly as she flipped the polaroid over to look at the photo on the other side. She knew what she was going to see even before she turned it. What else could it be? The Bad Man was revelling in his handiwork and he wanted to share it with Charlie.

The photo was a portrait. A shot of Kabir's ruined face. The hole where a short while before he had an eye. The gaping and bloody hole was not the worst of it though. It was the look of abject terror on Kabir's face. This was just for starters. There was much more and much worse to come.

Charlie could barely breath. She rolled and staggered out of the kitchen, not knowing where she was going nor what she was doing, she had to get out of that kitchen. She had hold of the bannister in the hallway, pulled herself around it and slumped on the lower steps of the stairs. She buried her head in her hands and cried.

She stayed that way for some time. When the crying had abated, the strength had left her. She felt light, almost as though her spirit was detaching itself from her body. There was no fight left in her. She'd thought about getting out there and driving her car. Chasing the Bad Man down. But what was the point? She was too late now and she would be too late by the time she found the Bad Man and Kabir. Besides, what was she going to do? How was she going to stop this monster?

Her thoughts went around and around in her head. They amounted to two thoughts. Mostly the same words over and over, but any break away thoughts were aligned with these two...

I'm sorry Kabir. I'm so sorry.

What am I going to do!?

I'm sorry Kabir. I'm so sorry.

What am I going to do!?

The letter box rattled and something landed on the floor in front of her.

Charlie stopped.

Everything stopped.

Someone had just pushed something through the letterbox.

The door was open. Charlie had left it open. The someone had chosen to use the letterbox all the same.

Charlie was suddenly alert. Her entire state changed. She sat upright, staring at the door and the white rectangle on the floor before her. There was only a moment's pause and then she was up on her feet and striding to the door, flinging it wide open to reveal...

Nothing.

She rushed down the steps and onto the gravel drive, her feet crunching loudly as she ran down the drive and to the pavement. She looked both ways before running right for twenty yards. Stopping and looking around her. Then back the other way to do the same, stopping. Looking. Searching.

Nothing.

She jogged back to the house, looking around her as she did.

She'd heard the polaroid posted, seen it land on the floor in front of her. How could someone post it and disappear like that?

She turned an entire circle in case whoever had posted it had tried to conceal themselves by the house.

No one was there.

As she walked back towards the steps and back into the house she paid heed to the sound of her footsteps in the gravel. There had been no sound outside the door before or after the polaroid was delivered.

There was no one here.

Charlie stepped back into the house. Looked on the floor for the polaroid. It wasn't there. Was her mind playing tricks with her? Where in the hell was the polaroid? She'd seen it! She growled in frustration and then froze as she spotted it. Four steps up on the stairs. In the spot she had been sitting. The polaroid had been placed carefully against the riser so it was facing her. The photo side was pointing at her.

It was the mouth of The Pipe.

She picked it up and looked more closely at it. The mouth of The Pipe was pitch black, but it you looked closely there were two pinpricks of light. Eyes. Something was looking out of The Pipe at Charlie. She could feel its eyes on her even as she peered at the image. A wave of something terrible. The eyes penetrating her and suddenly she was at the very edge of The Pipe. On the threshold of being drawn in.

Whispered voices. That stench.

Come to us! Come to us, Charlie!

Then the chanting.

Row, row, row
Row, row, row
Row, row, row
Life is but a dream
Row, row, row
Row, row, row
Row, row, row
Don't forget to
Don't forget to
Don't forget to
SCREAM!!

Charlie dropped the polaroid and stepped back. Breaking the spell. She was breathless and dizzy. She'd been at the mouth of The Pipe just now. The air had been different. Colder. And there was that stench. The breath of a carnal house. He'd been there. The Bad Man. Drawing her in. One more step and she would have been lost.

She looked down at the polaroid. It had fallen photo side down. There was a message scrawled on the back. No address or addressee this time though.

Don't delay!

Come visit today!

You'll have so much fun!

We know we are!!

Charlie's thoughts went to Kabir and the fun they would be having with him even now. Down in The Pipe. This sicko and The Bad Man.

The Bad Man.

Charlie had to go to the Bad Man.

She had to go to The Pipe.

14

Charlie shook herself and gritted her teeth. Two can play this game you sick bastard, she thought to herself as she walked back into the kitchen. She did her best not to acknowledge Kabir's eye as she found the drawer that contained the sharp knives. She selected three, figuring that she could decide which was best when the time came. That it also paid to have spares. She'd learnt that particular lesson twenty years ago.

Despite her best efforts, she could feel Kabir's eye on her all the same. She realised that she'd had a mild feeling of discomfort for a while now, That she felt as though she were being watched. Now it was intense. It couldn't be Kabir's eye though, could it? She glanced over to where she had left it. It was pointing right at her. She knew it's seeing days were over, that it was just so much meat and gristle now. But that did not stop her feeling like it was looking right at her. She backed out of the room. Noticing the sight of her breath as she did so. There was something very bad in here all of a sudden and the temperature of the room had inexplicably dropped. She felt her stomach flutter and a horrible clenching sensation, even as she fought the overwhelming fear rising up in her.

On trembling and unsteady legs, she made her way to Archie's garage. There was a light and she flicked it on absently as her hand found the switch.

She screamed as she saw what was on the other side of the garage, on the work bench. There was a dead animal that had been…

She looked away quickly, but the image of it was burnt into her mind. If anything, looking away and closing her eyes seemed to capture it there. Whatever it had been, it was now mangled and opened and…

THE PIPE

It was the cat.

Kabir must have put the cat in here. All the same it had given her the fright of her life. She almost laughed at the absurdity of it. It was alright. This was safe. This was the hideously butchered cat her friend had told her about. The friend who was even now suffering an even worse fate than this poor cat. She tried not to look at the cat's carcass as she rummaged around in the garage. She made several trips between the garage and her car, gathering provisions that may or may not be of use when she arrived at Dinsdale and finally caught up with the murderous and twisted scumbag and the Bad Man.

This was what she had to do. She had to go to Dinsdale and The Pipe and confront this evil. She would fight, if she could. She would certainly face this thing face on. Charlie was not going to go quietly.

She was doing this alone now though. She had planned on going to Dinsdale with Kabir. She had had a wing man. A partner who knew the score and who had her back. That had helped. She'd been complacent though, thought that they had time. They hadn't. Now it was just her.

She'd had a fleeting moment when she considered whether she could rope anyone else in on this. Charlie was the one who had dissuaded Kabir from involving the police, she was very aware of that. Kabir had rolled all too easily though. All the same, Charlie had been right. The same went for anyone else. Charlie wasn't close to anyone. Not close enough to come clean about what was happening, in the hope that they would also throw their hat into the ring. Stand shoulder to shoulder with her willingly in order to attempt to put a stop to this madness.

That was the problem though. This was madness. And now it was her own, personal madness. There was no one else to share it with. The only two people who understood had already met their end at the hands of this evil. However, Charlie wasn't quite right. There was someone else who understood. That was the person who had taken Kabir, the person who had taken those polaroid photos. He knew and he understood only too well. He wanted to share this with Charlie.

Perhaps he *needed* to share it with Charlie.

Charlie stopped in the hallway, about to leave Archie's house and drive to Dinsdale with the flimsiest of plans and therefore, by her reckoning, the flimsiest chances of success. But that was better than no chance at all, so she would cling on to some hope. She stopped in the hallway because something had occurred to her. What if the killer had chosen the order in which he killed the three friends? That made sense didn't it? So he had left Charlie until last. He seemed to be getting more proficient as he went along. Improving his craft.

An inner voice whispered words that made her shudder and lose heart.
He's getting stronger.
He's becoming more powerful.
Charlie was taking the fight to him as he was reaching the peak of his strength. Worse still, she knew that he wasn't alone. They'd all seen the Bad Man. The Bad Man was something *other*. She was going up against something more than a mere man. And on his home territory. The Pipe was the Bad Man's place. It was where he was most powerful.

He wouldn't be expecting Charlie to take the fight to him though and that gave her an edge. It gave her something and she'd take that right now.

"You sure you're up for this, girl?" Charlie whispered to herself as she stood in the doorway of Archie's house. She was looking down at her pathetically average and inconspicuous hatchback car. That was not the steed of a hero. If this scene were on a big screen right now, the audience would groan or even laugh. Maybe some would throw their popcorn or drinks at the screen having paid good money to see some action and here they were being short changed with the beaten up, cheap car they had learnt to drive in. They may have forgiven the choice of car, had the hero of the piece borrowed it and driven it at breakneck speeds through narrow Parisian streets, crashed it through market stalls and down a series of stone steps, eventually giving it so much abuse he sheared the back end off and driving the remaining half a car on two wheels, casually pulled up outside a hotel in a shower of theatrical sparks, stepping out of it without a scratch and dressed immaculately in his dinner jacket for a soiree dropped the keys in the dumbfounded concierge's hand. Of course, the now violently modified vehicle would never be seen again in the rest of the film, it was a problem for the poor concierge of the hotel to magic away.

The problem here was Charlie. She was no hero. She knew that. But there was that quote she seemed to remember hearing about a hero being someone who got other people killed. She seemed to be doing pretty well on that score, so maybe she was a hero, if only in that respect.

Charlie sighed and stepped out of the house, closing the door behind her. She trudged disconsolately through the gravel, feeling like a school kid who really didn't want to do this thing. She felt small and inept. She also didn't feel ready.

She'd been pushing herself. Knew that she had to forge ahead and keep going because were she to stop then she may not start again. She had already been caught procrastinating and that had not ended well. Now though, she saw the sense in pausing. She had loaded her car and it sat there waiting. Refuelled and ready to go. She'd even been sensible and brought water with her. She wasn't hungry. Couldn't eat. But she had to keep hydrated, that much she knew.

Right now it was dark and she sure as hell wasn't going to go bowling into Dinsdale Woods and The Pipe on her own, and in the dark. She was probably splitting hairs here, The Pipe was pitch black regardless of the time of day, but it made a difference to her and she needed as much as possible in her favour. She'd take daylight. That would mean making her way to The Pipe would be easier and less fraught. Yes, she'd take that.

She walked past her car. Patted it on the rear as she did. It may not be the steed of a super star, but it was hers and she needed it right now. She knew it would deliver the goods and get her to where she needed to be and that was alright by her. All of this was going to be difficult, but at least this next part of it would be in her own space and on her own terms. If she'd been gifted a hyper car or a rugged four by four she would have said thanks, but no thanks, she was fine with what she had. This car was hers and they knew each other well enough, she was comfortable with that. She managed a small smile as she thought about this, a career in the movies was over before it had begun, she'd just managed to piss everyone off. The sponsors offering her their very latest flagship model, the director of the film and the entire crew.

14

Then there was the audience. She'd already considered them rioting in the film theatre at the mediocrity and ordinariness she was intent on inflicting upon them and yet here she was, sticking to her guns. She felt good about that, it made her feel like she might actually know what she was about after all.

Because shit like this doesn't happen to ordinary people like me, does it? That was the bottom line. A variation on the potentially self-pitying; why is this happening to me? Perhaps Charlie's angle was more humble, she didn't think she was all that special, whereas the other angle inferred someone was too special for this horrible stuff to happen to them. She was in the spotlight though and this was now all about her. She was special after all. Of the billions of options open to this sicko, she was *the one*.

Why?

She crossed the road and carried on walking in that direction, leaving the pavement and walking a well-worn and sandy path that took her towards the sea. She was too wired to even try to sleep. Being near the sea was a good alternative right now. She had time to kill, so why not spend some of it by the sea. She'd barely paid attention to the sea previously. Too distracted by Archie's death. That's not to say she didn't spot the sea as she approached it. There was something about seeing the sea for the first time on a car journey that took her back to her childhood. A part of her childhood when they all together and they were happy.

That thought jarred her.

Billy.

She had a memory of sitting in the back of the car and the two of them being excited as her folks told them that the sea was going to appear any moment now. It had seemed like an age before it did. Charlie was about to complain to her parents, she was on the verge of calling her Dad a liar. They were miles away from the sea! There were only cars and houses and the occasional person walking along the adjacent pavement. The most interesting thing she'd seen since her father had announced the impending appearance of the sea was a dog. And as she had pointed it out to Billy it had concertinaed up and began pumping out the brown stuff from its butt.

Billy had giggled and the giggle had turned into an infectious laugh and they had both laughed heartily when Billy had exclaimed, "The dog was doing a poo!"

That was the year before he died. His penultimate summer on this earth. Then he'd been taken from her. Taken from all of them and left a Billy sized hole in their lives. In their hearts. Charlie could not understand how such a small person could leave such a big hole. Only it wasn't an empty hole. Calling it a hole missed the point. The point was the pain that rushed in to fill the space that he had left. The pain never left. It was the pain that Charlie's Dad could not deal with, so he joined Billy exactly a year to the day, and he left more pain behind. More pain and less people to deal with it. Now it felt like it was all Charlie's burden. That it always had been.

If Charlie was honest with herself, the second wave of pain that her father unleashed when he took his own life was not half as bad as the pain that Billy had left her with. She had wondered at this. Was it as simple as the smaller the person who died, the more concentrated the pain they left you with? She thought this might be a part of it, the rest was a case of Charlie having learnt about this pain and the coping mechanisms she could use to ignore it and compartmentalise it. It certainly wasn't because her Dad had *performed a selfish act.* Charlie had heard people say this of suicide and she did not agree, could not prescribe to their black and white and judgemental pronouncement on things they had no valid experience or knowledge of.

Billy's death had killed her Dad the same as cancer killed people. You could not see the damage it was wreaking as it found its way inside them and did its damage. That was how it worked. Maybe if you could see it, then the doc could do something about it. They said that didn't they? If only they had caught it earlier. As though, by catching it earlier it's progress could be halted. Charlie doubted it though. One way or another, her Dad's days were numbered once Billy died. Charlie knew it wasn't because he didn't love her. She thought it likely that had it been her who'd died instead of Billy the same outcome for her Dad was probable. She wasn't certain because there was no logic to life and how people dealt with things. She had grown up a lot over that first year after Billy's death and then her Dad had taken his own life and

14

she'd come to accept that *shit happens.*

Shit happens and you really don't know how you're going to deal with it until it does. You can say what you like about what you might do and some people talk a really good game, but until it happens to you, you have no way of knowing. You can kid yourself that you wouldn't countenance an intruder in your house, that were someone to break in, then you wouldn't be held responsible for your actions. Convince yourself that you would jump out of bed, take the stairs two at a time and tear the invader limb from limb. As there's seldom accounts of burglars torn limb from limb, Charlie's conclusion on this was that most people would stay tucked up in their warm and safe bed and rationalise any noise as the wind or an amorous wild animal out on the patio. They knew deep down what the reality was, but they figured that if they painted themselves another, easier one, then that would make the problem go away.

There was a lot of that. People did that more often than not in their lives.

Charlie was only partially lost in her thoughts as she followed the path and found steps down to the beach. There was a full moon undulating across the water. The waves were gentle. The sea was heaving as though it were a huge creature breathing contentedly. The sigh of the water lapping against the sand was calming. She could see enough by the moonlight to discern the divide between sand and water, so she was slightly surprised to find that she had plotted a course diagonally into the sea.

The water that enfolded her calves and seeped into her trainers was cold. Colder than it had any right being. It enlivened her though and she kept walking, tracking that bit further into the sea until it was pushing towards her knees. She carried on for a while like this. Going no deeper and remaining far enough in, that the water pushed against her and rose as high as her knees.

She couldn't remember the last time she'd paddled in the sea. In some respects, she'd grown up too quickly. In others she'd been frozen in time. Until now, she hadn't realised that she'd avoided the sea. It reminded her too much of Billy and the pain of losing him. She'd closed parts of her life down because she couldn't face the reminders of Billy and her Dad. They wouldn't have wanted that. They wouldn't have wanted her to miss out. The dead do not expect their living to stop the business of living, but often, the living mistakenly pay that price in any case.

15

Charlie was driving now. She'd walked for hours. Sat for a while to watch the reappearance of The Sun in her sky. Marvelled at how for a time, the warmth in the night had been drawn away in the same way the sea recedes before the waves crash forth. After a brief drop in temperature, The Sun had then got on with warming the new day.

She'd forgotten that temperature dip, thought that she should do this more often; be there to greet The Sun as she takes to her throne once more. The dawn. A new beginning.

Once The Sun was making its way above the horizon, Charlie knew that she could delay no longer. It was time. As she climbed into her car, she checked herself in the mirror, half expecting to see an altered reflection. She had changed. Everything had changed. Yet she looked exactly the same. That didn't seem right. She felt cheated somehow, as though her unaltered state was a reminder of her insignificance and the disinterest that the universe had in her plight. Yes, great evil was stalking the Earth, but it had always been this way. Justice and fairness were fine dreams, but they had no place in this world. They were mere fancies of a transitory race. Nature was cruel and the cruellest of jokes it had ever played was the creation of humankind. Humans had shown an aptitude for cruelty and taken it further than anyone could ever have imagined.

As she started her car, Charlie twisted the heater controls so they were turned up to their hottest and fiercest, splitting the jets of air between the screen and her feet. She opened her window a couple of inches. Before reversing and turning her car out of the driveway, she glanced at her upturned trainers – they were sat in the passenger footwell. She'd tipped the water out of them before getting in the car and stripped her socks off for good measure. She'd thrown them on the floor of the rear footwell behind her, thinking even as she did that they were probably best binned. An afterthought which was not listened to in favour of the old retort; well it's done now.

The majority of the journey from Archie's to Dinsdale was uneventful. Most journeys are just so, necessities that provide a transition from one place or state to another. The state of family and home to work being an all too common one. Trains and motorways seem designed to help facilitate a sameness that allows the mind to shut off and ignore the monotony of a journey repeated thousands upon thousands of times. Ignore it and it will go away. And it does just that.

Charlie took the motorway. It was the quickest and easiest option. Dinsdale was a mostly modern urban area. An overspill for towns and cities that were commutable via the motorway network. From the motorway, the sprawl of housing estates could be seen emerging from the land. The nearest houses had gardens that backed onto a field that met the motorway. The noise must have been constant and not a noise that was easy to get used to as although constant, it was arhythmic and went out of its way to be intrusive. It would always make itself known when it felt it was being ignored or risked being forgotten.

As Charlie saw the signs for the junction, things started to change. It had been all too easy to make her focus the here and now. She was driving on the motorway and the motorway was both familiar and unfamiliar. It could be a stretch of road almost anywhere in Britain. Mile after mile after mile of interminable and anonymous tarmac. She may as well have been on a treadmill staring at wallpaper.

Now though, she had to face reality. She was no longer in a never ending land of tarmacked limbo. She had been roughly shaken awake and been brought crashing back to reality. Her reality. She was nearing her destination and that destination just happened to be waiting for her. Despite the heat pumping out of the vents she was cold. She was entering an entirely different state now. As she indicated and pulled off the motorway she felt like she was falling. She'd always thought that there was no way back and she had never wanted to come back. This was a place from a past life and although she had not consciously vowed never to return. Not uttered that promise. It was made all the same. It wasn't that there was nothing for her here anymore, it worse than that. Much, much worse. There was something here for her and she did not want it. She had killed that version of herself the same as her Dad had killed himself, only she had been young and had the option to start over again. Build another life that chose to ignore this life. She could sacrifice those few years she had already lived and start again. Her Dad had not had that option, he was far too invested in the life he had built. Far too invested in her and Billy.

She saw that now. His Charlie had died too. He'd known that. Perhaps even seen that he was the last thing tying her to this place and a life that she had chosen to forget. By taking his life, he consigned this place to memory and once there, Charlie could deal with it as she wished. File away those memories that she did not want to revisit and reinvent herself as someone else.

She'd killed Billy and she'd killed her father. She was just too ignorant and self-absorbed to see it. You didn't need a knife or a gun to kill. Not most of the time. There were plenty of other ways to kill someone. Love was one way, or rather the withdrawal or corruption of it. You didn't have to know you were doing it. It wasn't done on purpose, but then lots of things weren't done on purpose. At least that was what we told ourselves.

Slowing the car as she pulled off the motorway was suddenly awkward and unnatural. She'd been lulled into a semi-soporific state and now her limbs weren't obeying the commands her brain was sending to them. She felt her pulse rise as the junction approached and the car wasn't slowing as much as it should. She needed to be here and she needed to be here right now! Something snapped into place at the last minute and her car skidded to a halt at the red light beside it. She noticed the driver in the sales executive car in the next lane looking across at her. He was agape at her smoking and screaming arrival at the junction. Only then did she understand how spaced out she had been. Seeing the look on the man's face seemed to herald in the smell of the burnt rubber and her perception of the positioning of her car. It was at a forty five degree angle to the stop line. She'd lost herself back there. She couldn't afford to be like this.

She smiled sweetly at the man in the car next to her. This wasn't a considered strategy, she felt the smile appear on her face and something about it seemed to do the trick. The man nodded at her as though to say; OK, that's alright then, all too willing to take the nice, neat and easy option.

Charlie had time to compose herself at the wheel while the lights decided when they would move through amber to green. She was slow and deliberate with her movements, allowing the sales man to get away before her. She felt the clutch bite and the car transport her towards Dinsdale. The sight of the place was both familiar and completely alien to her. She recognised it, but it wasn't the place that had been her childhood home. The place of her childhood had been extracted and hermetically sealed. She made frequent involuntary trips to that place in her dreams and it was a world away from where she was right now.

The terrible thing about that was that this Dinsdale was the alien place, not the Dinsdale of her dreams. Even when the majority of those dreams were nightmares. There was something so off kilter with the place she was entering right now that she was finding it difficult to breath. Her driver's side window was open, but all the same the air in the car's cabin was being sucked out and Charlie was struggling to draw a breath. She gasped and her vision blurred. Her head was no longer her own. She had to stop the car but didn't know how or where that was going to happen. She lifted off the throttle, felt the car slow. Heard the angry siren call of a car's horn, the driver not happy with her erratic driving. Her car was crawling, so she dropped the clutch and pressed the brake. Leaning forward and almost hugging the wheel as she struggled to stay conscious.

She stayed like that. Not daring to move, even as she experienced a return to normality. She supposed she'd suffered a panic attack, but it was more than that. A drastic and amplified version of someone walking over her grave. And it was a grave that she was heading towards far too quickly. She was going to climb into the very earth to face something that was not human.

15

She was walking to a place of death.

It knew she was coming. It was expecting her. The thing that had just happened. What she had experienced. It was the Bad Man turning his gaze upon her. He was near. He was watching intently.

The Bad Man was waiting for her.

16

Dinsdale. A northern town that had grown during a resurgence of industries and businesses across the North West during the eighties. The area had held its own in the nineties, more than held its own. It was on the up and up and this was proven in the way developments appeared from nowhere and were sold out before completion. Dreams were sold in this part of the world and they were delivered upon.

That was then. The then in question was the time Charlie had spent here. There had been an energy and a vibrance to the place. She remembered that now. The memory surged forth against the backdrop of a Dinsdale that had seen better days and was unlikely to witness days like that any time soon. Dinsdale had had the stuffing knocked out of it. It was a shadow of its former self and even The Sun seemed unable or unwilling to do anything about the shadow that was now cast upon it. The place was grey and dreary. It had lost its way and it was never going to find its way back.

All of this added to Charlie's feeling of foreboding. She was a stranger in a strange land. And right now, that stranger was huddled over her steering wheel causing an obstacle for the traffic coming into town.

Tap!

Tap!

Charlie looked up from her steering wheel, looking for all the world like she was raising her head from her pillow and would dearly love to have another hour's sleep. This wasn't a million miles away from the truth.

The man at the passenger window of her car had been walking his small, white Scotty dog, he was peering in at her, a concerned expression upon his

16

middle aged and well-worn countenance.

"You alright, love?"

Charlie's face lit up with recognition. The man's voice. His accent. That had an invigorating effect on her. This was the place. This was her place after all.

She nodded. Her head clearing. Managed a faint smile.

"Yes, I'm..." she began, "Thank you. That was lovely!" She brightened and with it so did her smile.

She waved and mouthed thank you again before pulling away into the morning traffic.

He watched her go, a puzzled expression now painting his face. All he'd done was ask if she was OK. He shrugged as she disappeared from sight and returned to walking the block with his dog.

She found that she was driving around Dinsdale almost aimlessly, but making a concerted effort to avoid Dinsdale Woods and her childhood home. She told herself that she was on a reconnaissance run. Casing the joint. The truth of it was that she didn't want to stop. Didn't know where to stop. She glanced down at her fuel gauge. It was still half full, but she knew that was a lie. That when the needle pointed halfway there was less than a half tank left.

"Contrary bitch," she whispered at the fuel gauge. She hadn't forgiven it for putting her through hell on the way to Archie's place.

Eventually, she pulled in at a cheap hotel. She'd driven past it twice, on the third occasion she made a last minute decision. Enough was enough. She wrenched the steering wheel and almost threw her car off the road and into the hotel's car park. It was done. She was stopping. She parked up and got out of her car.

The hotel was a large red brick house. It wasn't clear whether it had always been a hotel, purpose built like this, or reassigned from a rich family's dwelling to a hotel at some point in its history. Charlie doubted there ever would have been rich families in Dinsdale, but that was based on her limited and more recent knowledge of Dinsdale. She didn't know anything of Dinsdale's past. She supposed it should be part of her reconnaissance, research of Dinsdale. She'd looked up newspaper articles, but not information on Dinsdale itself. She supposed it would be a swift piece of work, there couldn't be much out there on Dinsdale. Dinsdale had specialised in unremarkable, even in its heyday.

Charlie entered the hotel and immediately found herself at the reception desk. Inside the hotel, the decor seemed to have been selected by someone who viewed the project as an opportunity to deck the interior out in the way they would have if this was their house. It was a chance to express themselves here with a good budget in a way that they may never be able to do in their own home. It should have been homely. It wasn't. For starters, nothing quite matched and that really didn't help on the homely front. It was also too busy. Whoever had spent the budget believed in spending it all until there wasn't a single penny left, which might have explained the cheap tat interspersed in the more tasteful and expensive décor. Those touches really brought the whole place down.

The man behind the desk greeted her with a smile that didn't quite reach his eyes, "Good morning, can I help you?"

Charlie wasn't ready for this and needed time to catch up with what was happening in this interaction. There was an overlong pause which gave the reception man time to raise an eyebrow and over emphasise an expression that already went beyond expectant. The looked helped convey the fact that the man had seen it all, several times over, and he was mighty tired with most of it, so if Charlie could just piss in the pot or get off it…

Charlie had now caught up and decided upon a course of action. She knew what she was going to say, but now she waited a few beats longer. She had time and the man sitting before her seemed supercilious, there was something about him that was annoying her. She knew that she shouldn't be doing this, but once, a long time ago, someone had drunkenly told her about *small victories*. There are many types of drunk and on this particular night, this guy was the sort of drunk who wanted to vent and he also wanted to show off. He wanted to tell the assembled that even when they may think they were better than him, he had already had the last word. Then he explained his approach to *small victories*. "You know that moment when you reach for something on your desk and it isn't where you thought you put it?" He grinned menacingly at everyone. He was enjoying his little revelatory moment, "No! Of course you don't!" He lowered his voice, "You haven't a clue. I know, because I watch you and your puzzled little face as you absently reach for that stapler and it isn't where you thought it was. Then you spot it just a little way from where you expected it to be and your little face lights up." At this point, everyone was pulling an approximation of the very face he had described. Only it was a variant. There was puzzlement in the faces arrayed around him, but everyone simply wondered about what he was saying, did he really do this? He continued, "I moved it! It's me! I've done it to you all! I've caused you a moment of mild inconvenience and scored my small victory and I always do it before any of you has a chance to get one over on me! I got there first!" He grabbed a fistful of air and pulled it towards him to signify his victory, "Yes!" He looked like a complete idiot.

Perhaps *small victories* are not the way forward, Charlie thought to herself, but sometimes, it cannot be helped. Someone starts a tussle and you get caught up in it, you make a stand and you retaliate. This was what she was doing in Dinsdale after all. Only the stakes were much higher. A hell of a lot higher. She wondered whether the principles were the same. The killers need to score points. Validate themselves in this way because the usual routes to validation were denied to them. Was Charlie dealing with the kid who was bullied at school? Or the school bully, who was invariably one and the same, the bullied graduating to meting out punishment to the kids that they could have best related to, but instead chose to hate. Because when it came down to it, they hated themselves. They looked in the mirror and they despised themselves. So easy then to move onwards and upwards until they were looking up to something like the Bad Man, an elevation of all the hate and hurt. A twisted form of perfection.

Charlie couldn't remember any kid at school who would fit this bill. But then, everything had been blurred out of focus when Billy had died. Those memories had been locked away and that made them all the more difficult to retrieve. Many of the best remembered memories have seen the light of day a number of times. They have been played with and rehearsed until they take on a life of their own. They are perhaps not the original memories, not what they once were. They've been interpreted and changed. They have grown into something more and something different.

The other reason for not remembering likely candidates from her school days was that the usual suspects were loners. They didn't mix well and most of their interactions were to inflict themselves upon individuals. Charlie hadn't been bullied. She hadn't been singled out and it had taken twenty years for her and her two friends to be targeted.

She found herself wanting to ask Kabir and Archie whether they remembered anyone who would fit the bill. Remembered that they were gone. She was alone in this endeavour. It was lucky that she had thought to bring her laptop. At least she had the internet and search engines.

Charlie smiled at the receptionist whilst her mind was exploring these points. Her smile was a response and created a holding position. The man couldn't do much with it. He had to return the smile, that was the rule here. Then he had to wait. She reached a convenient place in her thoughts.

"Can I have a room, please?"

"Have you booked?"

"No," Charlie doubted she needed to book, unless there was a World of Widgets convention taking place right now.

The man gave her a look. The look was tried and tested and given whenever a potential guest had not booked in advance. It was judgemental. A person who did not book ahead was not organised and they were therefore not successful. This behaviour also spoke of a lack of respect for this fine establishment. IF and that was a big IF, there was a room available then this wayward guest should feel very grateful indeed.

There was a room available.

There was always going to be a room available.

"Have I missed breakfast?" Charlie asked as the man booked her in.

He now selected from his extensive repertoire of disparaging looks *the idiot* and without further ado he gave it to her, "Madam," said in a way that was dangerously close to *madman*, "the breakfast included in the price is after you have slept in your bed. It is bed *then* breakfast."

Charlie smiled a smile that did not reach her lips, let alone her eyes. It was a set of face that countered the man's look, "Yes, but I would like breakfast now... *as well.*"

The man was not one for breaking with convention. He muttered something about this being highly irregular, then at an audible level, "I don't have the facility to do that here."

"OK…" Charlie looked askance knowing that any help from these quarters would be like getting blood from a stone.

Thankfully, the fates intervened and a member of staff chose this moment to appear.

"Ah! June! This lady wants to pay for a breakfast."

June stopped and stood, awaiting further illumination. The man waved at her like he was brushing dust vigorously off his counter, "Can you just… TAKE HER!"

June moved cautiously into action, as much to rescue Charlie as anything else. Leading her into a nearby room for breakfast. In all the confusion of the dysfunctional interaction, June hadn't grasped that Charlie was to pay for the additional breakfast and as the supercilious man was on reception when she left, Charlie would forget to mention it as she checked out.

Another *small victory.*

17

After a full English breakfast, that Charlie polished off swiftly, despite experiencing no hunger pangs, she went to her room via reception, smiling sweetly at the man as she went, and then sat on her bed with her laptop.

The first hits that Charlie found were for Dinsdale itself. They didn't really tell her anything she didn't already know, the place was a relatively new overspill for the nearby cities of Liverpool and Manchester and the various businesses and industries dotted around the North West. The eighties and nineties had been boom times and then the credit crunch had hit, knocking the already faltering town for six. The high street had suffered the same fate as many other high streets, leaving retail units unlet and those that survived were mainly charity shops, modern versions of pawnbrokers and betting shops. The pubs in the town centre were to be avoided at the best of times, but as darkness fell, fights were commonplace and knife crime had soared in recent years.

People were stuck in Dinsdale. Charlie couldn't help thinking that the vast majority of them were imprisoned behind bars of their own making. They could have broken out if they had truly wanted to, but staying was the easiest option, so they convinced themselves that it was the only option left to them.

Next, Charlie looked up her old school. She found a few sites and looked at them all. She had hoped for more photos, to scroll through the faces of her fellow pupils and stop when she saw the face of a killer. At that point, the kid in question would be a killer of small animals, yet to escalate their urges and kill larger prey. The photographs weren't there. No online year books.

17

Social media didn't make it easy to find people either. Besides, Charlie knew that this was all background. She may hit lucky with something that would help, but she wasn't going to open a link and see the killer revealed in full, technicolour glory. Life wasn't like that. The killer probably didn't have much of an online foot print. They may well spend quite some time online, but they weren't posting anything. They were watching. And they were waiting. They were good at that. Observing and choosing the right time to strike.

All the time she searched, articles on Billy's death suggested themselves. That and the tragic suicide of her father. She did her best to avoid them. Seeing the headlines and photos on the search page was too much for her. She didn't need reminders. She'd tried to forget and knew she never could.

She changed her search parameters. Looked at the general area and followed a string of threads until she was going back hundreds of years. Sometimes that happens, clicking link after link and disappearing down an online rabbit hole. Charlie had passed beyond the age of enlightenment to times when superstition, feelings and emotions were central not only to belief systems, but every day life.

Dinsdale didn't get a mention, so either it was too small at this time to be important, or it was known by another name. Several times The Seven Sisters were mentioned. This name rang a bell. Charlie had seen it as a child on road names and public buildings. It was a name well used in Dinsdale.

She opened a link that purported to tell the story of the Seven Sisters. Below the title and a couple of introductory sentences was an old sepia map that looked familiar. She opened her phone and the map app. Viewed Dinsdale, zoomed out and changed the view. There was enough there to tell her the Seven Sisters map was a very old map of the Dinsdale area. She read on.

The Seven Sisters may or may not have been sisters, many accounts insist that they were and that this was what made then so powerful. The story went that the sisters' mother was herself a seventh sister. No other siblings. No brothers. Seven sisters born of a seventh sister. There was much significance to this and the piece was keen to differentiate the seven sister legend to that of the seventh brother of a seventh brother, but it promised to come back to that later. No link to skip to. Read on and do this in the correct order. This was old school. Charlie liked that.

Unlike the seventh brother legend, it was not about the seventh of the sisters, it was about all of the sisters. The Seven Sisters were a sisterhood. They worked together and they stayed together. This was a part of who and what they were. As they grew up together, so did their powers. Powers for good. They healed not only anyone who came to them, but also the land. The whole area prospered as the sisters came into adulthood.

This period of prosperity and peace would not last, could not last. This is the way of things and the end of this period was a foregone conclusion. The sisters and the good fortune of the area were noticed and that drew attention. At first people came with good intentions, to settle and become a part of something that was self-evidently good. Then there was a string of suitors for the sisters. None was ever accepted. All were gently dissuaded of the notion that the sisters were available. They were for all intents and purposes nuns. Dedicated and wed to the land and the people. Nothing and no one could come between them and their purpose.

Some would not take no for an answer and these were driven from the village by the protective villagers and it was made clear that they should not return. That may or may not have been the beginning of the end. Men with poison in their hearts intent on the destruction of what they could not have. However it began, the seeds were ever present. Envy of other's success and happiness is the petri dish for conflict and war.

Soon the rumours were composed and spread. The Seven Sisters were witches. They had even named the village after themselves. This one act showed how vainglorious they were and the power and dominion they held over the villagers. No self-respecting man would allow this, but the populace of Seven Sisters were in the witches' thrall.

The tales of the witches of Seven Sisters and their wicked deeds were many and widespread. A remarkable number of people visited this small village and not only lived to tell the tale, but were privy to the most depraved and foul of deeds. Apparently, evil ran amok in the land and the cause of the evil, the well from which it sprang was the Seven Harlots. Why harlots? Well, they were known to dance naked in the wooded clearings and offer themselves to Satan himself. Some said that the villagers were the bastards from the sisters' many unions with the devil and his legion of demons.

Charlie marvelled at the success of these made up stories. Did anyone try to shout this nonsense down? Those who had dealings with the Seven Sisters and the women themselves readily demonstrating that they were not evil. Quite the opposite. That the evil was in the stories themselves and in those who thought it acceptable to make them up.

All of these hundreds of years later, nothing had really changed. Now there was a cult of opinion that required no substantiation and any dissent would be vilified and shouted down. Fake news was not a new thing and it was fake news that did for the Seven Sisters.

Or rather, it attracted the attention of a self-appointed Witch Finder. The piece found it interesting that there was no name to be found for this man. Only that he was the Witch Finder and that legend had it that he was the seventh brother of a seventh brother. In many cases, a seventh brother of a seventh brother was a good thing. He was imbued with powers that set him apart and made him wizard like. Man though has a dark side, and the seventh brother of a seventh brother can also have a dark side. These men become luison.

Charlie read on as the piece expanded upon the luison, a precursor to the story of lycans and werewolves, but those legendary and supernatural creatures were nothing compared to their ancient forebear. The luison was a foul and evil creature, dark and covered in the stench of death. The luison was the god of death.

The luison was the Bad Man.

Charlie shuddered at this discovery. She and her two friends had stumbled upon an ancient evil. An ancient evil that had killed her two friends. Now she was going to face down a foul creature that revelled in death, and she was going to face him alone, in the dark confines of The Pipe.

Enraptured by the story and the fate of the Seven Sisters, Charlie read on. She had to find out what had happened when the Bad Man had come to the

Seven Sisters. What he had done? She was sure it was terrible. She hoped that by knowing more about her enemy she would have an edge. Something that would make the difference when it came to it.

There were several versions of what happened once the Witch Finder was made aware of the Seven Sisters. The truth of it was that there was one version and one version alone, and the others were attempts to water it down and make it seem more real and less terrible.

Despite accounts that the Witch Finder had an army, this was not the case. He didn't need an army, he came alone. The Witch Finder was a persuasive man and with the force of his words alone he could bend an entire crowd to his will. The people around him were the tools of his trade. That said, there were accounts of a minion or a familiar. The accounts in this respect were confused. The Witch Finder and his familiar were sometimes swapped during an account. In others they were not differentiated; they were one and the same. It were almost as though the Witch Finder possessed the body of another.

The next part of the story was curious. The Witch Finder's arrival was foretold. Everyone knew that he was headed for the sisters and that when he arrived, they were done for. He travelled a straight line from the East coast of England, and wherever he stopped he found witches and executed them. The stories of the executions were blood curdlingly awful. The Witch Finder was a performer and executions were a highlight in the calendar for a people who had precious little to entertain them and distract them from a life of toil and hardship. These were dark times. But even these entertainment hungry and blood thirsty people agreed that this man went too far. Far too far.

You don't know the half of it, thought Charlie. She knew that the Witchfinder was in something of a hurry. These executions were a side show. He was eager for the main event.

She was right. He made remarkably good time. There were stories of his steed. A huge, midnight black horse with red hot coals for eyes. It never tired and it did not slow however far he went and however hard he flogged it.

The Witch Finder was in the North West in a matter of days. He could

17

have been in the village and meting out what went for justice the day after that. But he chose not to enter the village, instead he charted a route around that village and just happened to find a witch in each of the seven stops he made around the Seven Sisters.

The ends that these seven women met were particularly gruesome. They were all flayed alive. Some said that the proof of their evil was that they did not die, even when parted from their skin. Not for days. They lingered even after he opened them up on the third day of their torture and they eagerly consumed the parts of themselves that he offered up to them. Towards the end of the third day, the Witch Finder would place the witch upon a stout sharpened branch of at least seven feet in height. Gravity would do the rest. That and any struggling that the witch was capable of. The struggling hastened their end and was a mercy as the spike travelled up through them impaling them further and further.

This section ended with a dire warning. The fate of the Seven Sisters was to be worse than that of the seven witches. Much worse. The fate of the witches around the Seven Sisters was a warning and it served as a warm up for the Witch Finder.

18

It was nearing the end of a misty autumnal day. A day where the mist had never really left the land, lifting a foot or so from the ground at best, but lingering throughout the day. Now as the day neared its end, the mist was becoming more substantial and the temperature dropped, spreading a dread chill throughout the mists.

The villagers had known something was coming. The sisters had fore told it. They were wise in these things and knew eventually that this time would come. Then there were the stories. Recently the stories had stopped for one very simple reason. The Seven Sisters had had no visitors. No one had passed through these parts for these past few weeks. So now the villagers knew something was coming. They could feel it. They were under of a siege of sorts and even those minded to leave the place and avoid the unpleasantness that was imminent could not. There was nothing physically restraining them from leaving. Nothing prevented them from sneaking off in the night to avoid being seen and the shame and recriminations of deserting their friends and kin. But those who had set out on this course of action had soon abandoned their plans. The dark was deeper and closer than they had ever seen it. And it watched them. It goaded them. They could hear it calling to them and knew if they were to step further into it, to leave the relative safety of the village, they would be done for. Whatever was out there waiting for them was hungry and it would feed eagerly upon them.

In the three days prior to this day, the noises began. At first there were snatches of sound as the villagers went about their business. They would stop suddenly and cock their ears, they had heard something strange and awful, but now that they attended to it, there was no further sound. It was not gone. They knew that much and they had heard the single, terrible sound clearly.

The frequency of these sounds increased. Especially at night. The falling of the night heralded louder and more terrible sounds. There was something of the wolf about them and all the while they drew nearer, became louder. They encircled the village and prowled. They grew more insistent. Hungrier. More feral. They promised violent death.

On this day, the mist closed in and dropped down onto the land, shrouding it. The sounds stopped abruptly, which this cessation all other sound ended. There was an ominous silence that fell upon the village, making its isolation complete.

Then the Witch Finder walked in as though it were the most natural thing to do. Behind him, leading his horse was a slight man with a stoop and an odd gait to his walk. This man had a nervous energy about him, his gaze darted from place to place, always searching for something no one else was able to see.

The Witch Finder wore dark clothing and a cloak with its hood up. The only impression to be had of him as he strode into the village was that he was dark. He brought some of the darkness that had encircled and besieged the village with him.

There was no reception for the two men. No one gathered in the centre of the village to greet him. He was however watched from each and every dwelling that he passed. The Witch Finder came to a stop in the centre of the village and looked about him. Despite the mist, he seemed able to see everything around him and his eyes came to rest on a particular hut, as they did, he strode forth and entered the dwelling. There were two short screams that were cut off swiftly and abruptly. The Witch Finder emerged from the hut dragging a small boy of about eight or nine Summers and walked back to the centre of the village. No one from the hut followed him. Later, both of the boy's parents were to be found with their necks so badly broken their heads had partially left their bodies and lay twisted at grotesque and unnatural angles, their faces were the worst of it. They were pulled into a horrible rictus as though they had seen the devil himself.

Some said that they had.

He pushed the boy into the arms of his companion and this was when he spoke for the first time.

"You have *all* been found *guilty!*" He spoke loudly yet clumsily, as though this language was alien to him. The words carried throughout the village and there was a wet, rasping quality to them. The delivery of this statement was as frightening as its meaning.

The eldest of the Seven Sisters stepped out from the mist. Her white clothing in stark contrast to the Witch Finder's. All of the sisters wore light colours and today she wore a dress of the purest white. "There is no need for this," she said clearly to the Witch Finder, but her gaze was upon the small boy.

"There is every need!" retorted the Witch Finder. He raised a hand and his minion slit the boys throat from ear to ear. So deep did the wicked knife cut that the boy's head tipped backwards and hung redundantly from the back of his neck.

The boy's blood spouted forth. The Witch Finder turned on his heel with inhuman speed and buried his head in the wound, his companion cackling in glee as his master fed.

Upon seeing this, two things happened.

First, the remaining six sisters came forth and offered themselves in the vain hope that the villagers could be saved.

And then, seeing their opportunity, several of the villagers ran from the village in a blind panic. There was the sound of pursuit. Snarling. Cries and screams. Retched and pitiful sounds punctuating by snapping and tearing. Then the complete and ominous silence returned.

The message was clear, none would escape and no one would be spared.

Nonetheless, the sisters went willingly and offered themselves up in an attempt to save the villagers and by the following day they were arranged in a circle in the centre of the village. Pinned to stakes with long and vicious nails. They say that even as the nails were hammered through them, none of the sisters made a sound. Throughout their torment, there was no cry of

18

pain nor a plea for mercy.

The nails the Witch Finder used were sharpened along their sides so they had knife like edges. They were coated in a poison which prolonged death and heightened pain. The Witch Finder was skilled in his trade.

The sisters were all arranged so they were looking inwards, into the circle. Once the Witch Finder was satisfied that they had all been secured, his companion led the villagers into the centre of the circle. They were instructed to dig. At first they thought they were digging their graves. Their graves and the Seven Sisters' graves. The Witch Finder commanded them to continue even as the single hole went deeper than the tallest of them. Deeper and deeper they dug and still it was not enough. They were not allowed to stop. They dug until the job was done or they were done. Several of the older villages collapsed with exhaustion, when this happened, the minion would drag them from the hole and open them up with his wicked curved blade and the Witch Finder would feast upon them as they died.

The minion warmed to his work and each subsequent villager was opened up in new and intricate ways, more flourishes of the knife and greater obscenities were visited upon each of the villagers. The stronger of the villagers redoubled their efforts in an attempt to reach the end of the back breaking work and spare the weaker of the villagers such a hideous end.

It took two days before the work was done and it was obvious when the end came.

The diggers at the vanguard yelled up from the deep hole. They had dug through to a hole in the earth. There was some sort of cave here.

Upon hearing this news, the Witch Finder threw his head back, looking up into the night sky at the full moon and gave forth a terrible howl. His hood encased head was exposed for the first time and what the villagers saw chilled them to the bone. This was no man. This was nothing of the Earth.

His companion danced gleefully around the edge of the hole until, upon a nod from his master, he leapt into it and herded the remaining inhabitants of the village into the darkness of the cave they had discovered.

The Pipe, thought Charlie. That was The Pipe. They dug until they uncovered the ancient and evil tunnel that she knew as The Pipe.

Nothing was ever seen of those people again. The ones who had dropped during the excavation were the lucky ones.

This left the Seven Sisters and the Witch Finder. For the next six days he defiled them. He entered them every way imaginable and in other ways unimaginable. He opened them up and tore at them and all the while they bore witness to what he had done as they hung suspended on knife like nails. Their blood seeping into the earth around the hole that led down into the very depths of hell itself.

On the sixth day, the Witch Finder looked upon what was left of the Seven Sisters. Almost unrecognisable as the beautiful young women they had once been. Barely clinging to life. Their silence during all the horrors that had been visited upon them was miraculous and eerie.

"It is done," said the beast as he stalked from one to the next, raking them with a claw to illicit a response or reaction. All he received were solemn gazes.

He looked across at the eldest sister, adjudging her to be the leader of the group, she was after all the eldest and the first to have stepped forth to meet him, alone. His assumption was that she was also the most powerful and the one he must begin with, for there was power here, even after everything he had visited upon them, these seven were powerful. He wondered at why they had been so meek and had surrendered so easily to him. Only now did he wonder that, as he stood within the circle eyeing their broken bodies.

He swaggered across to the eldest sister, "I will start with you," he hissed in her face, black spittle landing on her cheek.

She smiled in reply.

"Why do you smile? Do you seek to mock me, even as you lose?"

She laughed even though it pained her to do so. "Lose? Have you not realised what you have done?"

He looked at her curiously, not comprehending her meaning.

She whispered something so quietly he did not hear it. Although something of what she said still hit forth. He stiffened. Had he miscalculated? Had he underestimated these women?

He leant forward, "What did you say?"

18

Her eyes flickered with the effort of speaking. The very effort of defiance had visibly weakened her, but she whispered the two words to him all the same, *"our blood..."*

He looked down at the ground beneath her and saw the stain of her blood on the ground.

"No!" he gasped.

"Yes!" said a powerful voice behind him, strength and defiance aplenty from across the hole.

He span on the spot. The smallest and the youngest of the sisters was staring at him intently and she was moving...

"You took our maidenhead on this sacred ground, you fool!" She was pulling away from the stake. Regardless of the pain and the damage she was inflicting upon herself, she was pushing herself along the blades of the nails that had impaled her and she was succeeding in freeing herself. That should not have been possible. It wasn't possible. The wounds inflicted upon these women were grievous and fatal.

The Witch Finder glanced around him. The six other sisters where quietly chanting incantations and their strength was flowing through the seventh sister of a seventh sister. He could see the power flowing into her and lighting her up.

"See the circle you created with our blood!" she said triumphantly as she walked slowly over to the Witch Finder, "We waited and waited until our blood had mingled and formed the circle that would entrap you. A trap of your own making."

The Witch Finder looked around the circle, the dark blooms of blood had indeed edged out until they all touched. The circle was complete. There was no point at which the blood had not joined.

"You did this!" she was raising her voice to be heard over her sisters' incantations, "You used your power against us and we accepted it and joined it with our own. Remember this day. Remember what *you* did. Do not forget as you languish in the hole that you dug for yourself!"

She had closed the distance between them. The light within her even brighter and pulsating with every one of her heartbeats. A heart she shared with her six other sisters. They were as one.

"No! This cannot be so! You bitch! You fucking bitch!" he raised a hand to smite her. Nothing and no one could stand in his way. He would not allow it. Before he could bring down his claws on her and tear her apart she stepped forward and encircled him with her arms.

They stood like that. Two halves. The intense, bright light of good on one side and the dark of hell and nothingness on the other. His raised hand forgotten. Frozen in place. His power diminished with the shock of the contact and the sudden knowing of what he had been tricked into doing.

Trapped.

His face contorted into hatred and rage and he brought both arms around to complete the embrace, sinking his long, vicious claws deep into her sides.

"Yesssss!" was her last word.

He had not learnt. He had gone with his rage. His entrapment required her sacrifice and he had done exactly what she wanted of him.

They fell.

Tumbled from the edge of the hole, down into the confines of The Pipe, never to be seen again.

None of the inhabitants of the Seven Sisters were ever seen again. Inexplicably, only the ruined bodies of the villagers killed during the digging of the hole were found. Of the remainder of the villagers and the Seven Sisters, there was no sign.

Following those dark days, no one resettled the area and the settlement of the Seven Sisters fell into disrepair, then nature took over and the woodland crept over the spot where the sisters were sacrificed and the villagers were massacred.

Charlie finished reading the story and thought about The Pipe, she had previously wondered how old The Pipe itself was. The first part of The Pipe was old brickwork. This couldn't have been more than a couple of hundred years old. The brickwork had blended into stonework and then the stonework had faded into one, constant piece of rock. A long, descending cave, that was as old as the Earth itself. As old as heaven and hell.

If there was any truth in the story of the Seven Sisters, which Charlie

18

thought there was, then The Pipe was a portal to somewhere very bad and it was the lair of the Bad Man. It was also a cage. The sisters had managed to trap the Bad Man in The Pipe before, surely it was possible to do that again?

Reading the story had given Charlie hope. She knew her enemy now and she knew something of what could be done. Something of what must be done.

19

Somehow, after reading the story of the Seven Sisters, Charlie had drifted off to sleep. She hadn't thought it possible, but she woke with the open laptop discarded to one side of the bed and at some point she'd rolled over with her back to it. She glanced at her phone, it was early evening. She had caught a few hour's sleep. She wasn't sure whether she felt better or worse for having slept. She settled on feeling no worse than she had before her sleep.

Snatches of dreams came to her as she sat on the edge of the bed rubbing her eyes and coming fully to wakefulness. She had been dreaming of The Pipe, but of her dreams she recalled little else, she thought that was probably for the best. She was grateful for the rest and now that she was more wakeful, she was feeling rested. She felt better, if that were possible.

She stood and padded to the en suite bathroom, cleaned her teeth, glancing at her reflection and noticing how tired and worn out she looked.

"The vampire panda eyes look good on you kiddo!" she said to the other version of herself with the dark rings around her bloodshot eyes. It smiled back at her through the toothpaste. The white foam served only to make her look rabid.

As she finished at the sink she turned and without thinking began running a bath. She heard the sound of the running water, stared at the two jets churning the surface of the bathwater as the water level climbed. She poured the complimentary bubble bath under the taps and was satisfied to see the bubbles proliferating and moving across the surface of the water. She tested the water. It was warm, but not warm enough. She stopped the taps, stripped

19

and slipped into the bath. Once sitting, she leant forward and turned the hot tap gradually until it was gently topping the bath up and increasing the temperature. She sat away from the business end of the bath and gauged the temperature with her feet, waiting for it to get to a point that was almost beyond baring. She stopped the flow from the hot water tap using her right foot and swished the water around, mixing the very hot water with the pre-existing warm water. The temperature of her bath was just right. She looked around the bathroom, the mirror was covered with condensation from the now steaming bath. She sighed as she slipped under the bubbles to soak, immersing herself entirely for a short while, then pushing her head upwards so her bubble coated face was above the surface.

Charlie lay like that for a long while. She wished she'd taken her paperback out of the overnight bag in the adjacent bedroom, but then it was unlikely she could have mustered the necessary focus to read. That would have been frustrating, getting to the end of page after page knowing she hadn't taken the words in, her mind instead moving over and through other thoughts and not allowing her to escape the looming horror that awaited her. Not allowing her to escape her fate even for a blissful hour in the bath.

As it was, she managed to zone out and relax. The water was cleansing and soothing and she sighed several times as she let it cocoon her. She did not move for quite some time, and when she did, she slowly slipped her hands over her body, one after the other. It was a lazy effort at cleaning, or at least that was what she told herself as she embarked upon the slow, languorous movements. She was enjoying herself just a little too much to stop, even when she was certainly clean enough. Her hands lingering, no longer a part of her as she closed her eyes and abandoned herself to her gentle and building pleasure. The water and bubbles adding a certain something, making everything feel silky smooth as touched and stroked herself.

Charlie took her time, as she often did when she was in the bath. Elsewhere was different. Sometimes the pace was frenetic – she needed the release and would not wait, her movements fast and her body jerking in response. Now though she was barely touching herself. Teasing and playing with her wet body. Her mind drifting as her pleasure built. She took her time and held herself back allowing a gradual build up to the end.

She could almost feel him on top of her. The weight of the water was now his. He slid upwards over her and on top of her and he was slowly slipping inside her as she felt the weight of him on her. He moved gently, rhythmically, taking his time. She bit her lower lip as she abandoned herself to the pleasure of it all. Fighting the urge to go faster, holding back, knowing it would be better. She was past that particular point, the point where everything else was unimportant and this was all there was. She gave herself over entirely to her pleasure. She was so near now. So close. With every pulsing moment, every loud and glorious heart beat she felt so close. Nearly there, but not quite. Possibly the next heartbeat, if not then the one after that, yet her pleasure carried on building. She was panting, her breathing as intense as the pleasure. It was growing more and more real. She could feel him. She gasped. Imagining him inside her. She gasped with each pulse. Then, as her gasps should have drifted towards groans and moans she gasped in shock. The weight on her was increasing. She was being pushed downwards. She could feel her head going under the surface. She pushed back, fighting the force against her, gasping again with the effort of it. Panic building as the inexplicable weight on her pushed harder, forcing her down into the water. Confused, her body betraying her. Her pleasure continuing to build even as she struggled. Her body wasn't her own now, not completely. Selfish; it wanted to reach the pinnacle of its pleasure and it would not be denied. It had come to far now and nothing else mattered.

She was thrashing now, fighting whatever it was that was pinning her. Her head was under the water, so she couldn't cry out. Her eyes bulged, sightlessly. Open and yet unseeing. Why could she not see? Darkness. She was shrouded in water and darkness. The more she struggled, the more pressure was against her and the more she moved against him. He went deeper and harder and she couldn't stop. She couldn't give in, she had to fight or she would die.

Then it was happening, she was thrashing around in the water, trying to break the surface, fighting for her life even as the pleasure rose from inside her.

19

No! No! I can't, she thought as she felt the huge wave of pleasure rising up from within and then it overwhelmed her. She held what little breath she had as she lay under the water and abandoned herself to wave after wave of pleasure. It grew in intensity with each wave. She stopped fighting, her body rigid and convulsing. She didn't think it would stop, not until she was finished. This was her end. Sex and death, so closely related.

"Aaaah!" a rasping sound as she broke the surface, suddenly released and pulling in a life giving breath.

She forced herself up to a sitting position. Drawing in deep breaths and shuddering with the effort. What the hell had just happened?!

Another shudder, this one reminding her of some of what had just happened. An aftershock of pleasure. Then she was shivering. The bath was stone cold and she could see every exhalation of her breath. The room itself was freezing. She climbed quickly out of the bath and lunged for a towel, wrapping herself swiftly and stumbling out of the bathroom. Her bedroom was comparatively warm, she felt the difference immediately. It took her a while to warm herself nonetheless.

As she dressed, she wondered at what had just happened. It had been *him* she was sure of it. It had begun as a dream, a fantasy of someone else that was perhaps flavoured by the stories she had been reading and thoughts of the Seven Sisters, but then it had taken on a life of its own, almost as though she had inadvertently summoned the Dark Man.

She would have to be careful, if it was possible to summon him with careless thoughts she would put herself in danger. The fact that he could see her thoughts was bad enough. She wondered how much of what had just happened was her and whether he really could have drowned her. She doubted he could do that, but it had been a close run thing.

Charlie checked the time now that she was dressed. It was five p.m. so maybe today was not the day that she would go down into The Pipe and confront the Dark Man and his twisted companion. She would go tomorrow, late morning so that she was entering The Pipe around noon. That felt right. A good time to do the deed. And a time of her choosing.

Now, she would go for a walk. Explore the local area on foot and find somewhere to eat. She felt hungry now and there was sure to be somewhere she could find for a meal. She didn't fancy eating in the hotel, needed to get out and stretch her legs, feel the sun on her face and get some fresh air.

She checked herself in the bedroom mirror before leaving her room. Despite her near death experience she looked better for her bath. If anything, she felt enlivened for what had happened. She had fought the Bad Man and survived. She tried not to downplay it too much, but that had been a shadow of the Bad Man and his companion was not to be underestimated. She was outnumbered two to one. And that was the good news.

As Charlie grabbed her room card from the wall socket that enabled the room's lights, she spotted something on the floor by the door. She thought nothing of it at first. It was likely a note about breakfast the next morning. If she wanted breakfast in her room, tick the relevant boxes and leave the card at reception. She picked it up in order to give it a cursory glance and place it on the side out of the way.

She froze.

It was a polaroid.

She could feel the unmistakeable shiny surface between her fingers and thumb even before she saw what it was. She had turned it so she was holding it photo side up. The image was busy and confused and she took a while to discern what it was that she was seeing. It was dark and layered with shadows, but as she focused she could see there was a mess of flesh and gore. A pile of butchered and defiled bodies, intermingled and twisted together in a way where it was impossible to see where one ended and another began. Mostly, the bodies were those of animals, the bones and carcasses too small to be human. Here and there though, Charlie swore she could see something human.

In the foreground was a hooded man tied to a chair. She could tell it was a man as he was naked and bleeding. His skin seemed dark.

Could it be Kabir?

Her eye was caught by something above Kabir. Something protruding from the hideous pile of defiled corpses. Something familiar. But how? What was…

19

Charlie felt her gorge rise at the same time as recognition dialled itself in.

Archie. It was Archie's face. He was the centrepiece, emerging from the sculpted dead things. His eyes had been removed and his mouth was opened impossibly wide. As though...

As though he were a drowning man, breaking through the surface of corpses. Fighting to gain a lifesaving breath before being dragged down by the dead and consumed by them, joining their ranks.

Charlie dropped the polaroid and barged into the bathroom. Falling to her knees before the toilet and puking violently. Crying tears of pain and rage. Convulsing. Hands bunched into fists.

She found her feet and ran the cold water tap in the sink. Cleaning herself up, splashing her face with the cold water for good measure.

"Bastard!" she muttered to herself as she left the bedroom.

She looked down at the polaroid she had dropped, not wanting to touch the vile thing again. It had fallen photo side down.

He's still alive!

Writ large on the back in that awful writing. No address or addressee. There was no need for that now. They were all friends here.

20

Kabir was still alive.

Charlie felt numb at learning this news. She had dallied and delayed and needlessly put Kabir through untold torture and pain. Did she dare believe that this was the truth of it? Could Kabir still be alive? She had to believe it was true and she had to do something about it, right now.

Idiot, Charlie, idiot she thought to herself as she stormed from her room.

At the reception desk she slowed. The same supercilious man was sat at reception. He raised his head to see who was approaching and gave Charlie a look; *oh, it's you*. She slowed and eyed the man, thinking. He gave her a curious look wondering what she was cueing up, but she had thought better of it. She had been about to ask him if he had seen anyone just now, but she doubted anyone had seen the person who had delivered the polaroid. She doubted anyone had delivered any of the polaroids. There was some weird shit going on here and in any case, identifying the messenger would be of little use to her now. It was too late for that. Right now she needed to go and find her friend and if she was lucky, save him.

She still had time. Somehow, miraculously, she had time. Kabir had time.

Charlie picked up her step and left the man at reception wondering about his odd guest. They were all varying degrees of odd, but this one stood out. She was particularly odd and something about her frightened him. Right now, Charlie would be pleased to glean this, especially when it came to this annoying man.

She climbed into her car and drove. She didn't have to think about what

20

she was doing or where she was going, she just drove knowing this part would take care of itself because she was focused on what she needed to do.

Time. It wasn't a miracle at all was it? It was the Bad Man. He wanted her to come to The Pipe now and he knew how to make that happen. She was dealing with evil and she had to prepare herself for anything, it was just as probable that Kabir was already dead, or that the Bad Man was intending to kill Kabir as Charlie showed up.

He would make Charlie watch. She would watch and know that she was next. That he was saving the best until last.

Charlie had to be prepared for anything and ride out whatever happened. All that mattered was that she stop the Bad Man. She'd run away twenty years earlier and lost her little brother Billy and her Dad. She'd left that gate open. She had to go back and right those wrongs. She had to stop him and she would.

* * *

As Charlie neared her destination and caught sight of Dinsdale Woods, she was transported back to that fateful day. The woods themselves had not changed. Now though, she knew more about the woods themselves, as well as the evil secret that they contained. She knew that were she to have a drone or find higher ground, there would be seven tall trees which stood head and shoulders above the other trees; the Seven Sisters. Trees planted to commemorate the Seven Sisters who had sacrificed themselves so that others may live.

Charlie supposed that she had expected the woods to be different. After all, Dinsdale was. It was darker and less vibrant, it lad lost the lustre of an idyllic childhood. Worse than that, it was decaying. The whole place was a shadow of its former self.

The woods were the same as they ever were though, and as Charlie stopped the car she remembered the many times the three of them had adventured here. And all of the other golden times. Riding their BMX bikes around the local area and finding places they could call their own. Places to adventure in. Death defying jumps for their bikes, the blue rope tied to a tree branch over the brook. A stick tied to the end for them to stand or sit on; their Tarzy. Named after Tarzan, but this fact had escaped them. To them it was just their Tarzy, it was a name handed down from kid to kid and had started life way back when Johnny Weissmuller was plying his trade as the loin clothed bedecked jungle based hero, swinging from tree to tree on vine ropes whilst yodelling a call which mustered all the animals in the jungle. The animals all understood that call and they always came to Johnny-Tarzan's aid. Charlie could do with a bit of that right now.

This part of the woods was familiar to Charlie. It was her woods, it was their woods. Their shared space. Their home. If only they had stayed here and not pushed on. They had gone too far and paid the price for their trespasses. Until then, they had got away with a dousing, a bruise here and a graze there. None of them had broken a bone and they had been oblivious to germs or concussion. They'd ridden their luck, but that was all part and parcel of a childhood lived well. In their case their luck had run out when they stepped into The Pipe and they'd spent the last two decades thinking they'd gotten away with it when all they were doing was living on borrowed time.

Charlie leant into the boot of her car and gathered her provisions, unloading her overnight rucksack and filling it with items she thought may be useful in The Pipe. She placed a torch in each of the two side pockets. Separate and easily to hand. She'd learnt something from that day. She was a little more prepared. How much use this preparedness would be, she did not know. She would find out soon enough.

She threw the rucksack over her shoulder, for all intents and purposes a woman going for a walk in the evening sun. Nothing at all unusual here. She wished that it were so. Breathing in deeply she could smell the woodland. A beautiful aroma, promising much on a lovely Summer's evening.

This was a return, not only a return for Charlie to this particular place but that of a modern human being going back to a place that made much more sense than the concrete jungle that was supposed to be home. Here was life, true life, not an illusion of life. A place to become centred and belong.

Charlie could not deny that feeling. With the sun on her face and that fresh aromatic air, this was the place to be. Despite her intended destination she felt better for being in this place. This space belonged to the Seven Sisters, this was what they gave their lives for. The woods that encircled The Pipe were sacred and filled with good. Charlie could feel it. She somehow felt bigger. Bolder. She could do this. She must do this.

She had to do this for Kabir. For herself and for Archie, Billy and her Dad.

She nodded to herself and marched into the woods. A short way along the path she realised she hadn't locked her car, she did not even slow. Leaving the car unlocked was not a problem in her scheme of things. It no longer mattered. All that mattered was her in the here and now and what lay ahead of her.

As she went deeper into the woods her pace picked up gradually, the change was not noticeable but at some point she was running. The path was narrow, but the woodland did not encroach all that far. Low lying plant growth brushed her shins as she ran. The dappled light streamed over her face as she went, causing an illusion of immense speed. She ran and ran abandoning any pretence at decorum, giving herself over to the act of running and nothing else. Her legs pumped and she leant into it, almost stumbling several times but never slowing, falling was OK. Falling was a part of it and that was what awaited her as she crashed through the line of trees and into the clearing, launching herself at the ground and rolling as her legs gave way. She lay on her back in the long grass and she laughed. Staring up into the blue, cloudless sky, bordered by the tree branches she laughed and laughed, wheezing through the laughter from the exertions of running for all she was worth. She was the ten year old Charlie and this was the most fun she could have. To race through their special place and give herself to her rampant imagination. She could be anything. And right now, she was waiting for her fellow adventurers, only…

Her laughter dissolved into sobs and she gave herself over to her grief. Her grief for her two fellow partners in crime, her grief for Billy, her grief for her

Dad and her grief for her life. For herself most of all. For a life that she had only now realised had been in limbo, she had been unable to live her life and move on because it wasn't fair.

It wasn't bloody fair!

After the crying subsided, she lay there for a while, eyes wide open, but seeing nothing. She could just lay here and wait for the end. She didn't doubt that were she to lay here for long enough then the end would come to her. That wasn't in the script though. She would be cheating if she took that option. She thought of her Dad. No, that was different. That was entirely different. If he'd had another option, Charlie knew he would have taken it.

She got up, brushing herself off. Noting the green grass stains on the knees of her jeans. She thought of that day and Archie bowling her over. The day a part of all three of them died. She looked up at the sky once more, drawing a deep breath and noting how the light was a little less intense and the air cooler.

Time to go. She'd had her fun.

Almost at the tree line that would see her in the darker, thicker and inhospitable woods something made her turn. Directly behind her was a thick, tree trunk. Her eyes went from the base and up along its length. Taller than all the surrounding trees she saw it for what it was. One of the Seven. She walked across the clearing until she was at the foot of the tree. Gently lowering her head against the bark of the trunk, she slipped her arms around it, barely managing to span its diameter, she rested against the seventh of the sisters and closed her eyes.

And she was there.

There on the final day of the sisters' lives. She felt the power and light coursing through her and the seventh sister of a seventh sister spoke quietly in her ear. Told her things that she needed to know. Gave her the strength to carry on and do what she must do.

21

Entering the dark part of the woods was not as bad as Charlie had anticipated it to be. She was doing this on her own, but now she no longer felt alone. Before now, she had been worse than alone, the hole that she carried with her, the absence and loss created a void within her and it made it difficult for her to form attachments. She could not afford to lose anyone else.

Now she had been touched by the sisters and something had changed. She had been filled. She had an inner strength. She had purpose. And of course, she was bigger. Her path through the dark woods was difficult and the dense woodland stifled the light, the atmosphere itself was thick and oppressive, but she pushed through and she did not falter.

The distance to The Pipe through the thick foliage was not anything near what Charlie had remembered. She was disappointed to find herself at The Pipe's entrance all too soon. Her concerns about not finding it were unfounded. The Pipe was waiting for her, it would not make this part difficult. After all, it wanted her.

She stood there, recreating that pose of her at the mouth of The Pipe. Turning on her heel, she moved a full circle taking in her surroundings, half way through the circle she saw none of the path she had only now charted. The way back would be much more difficult. There was a constant rustling sound and an underlying, deep creaking. The woodland was closing in. It grew darker. The woods had opened to invite her in, now they were closing ranks, emphasising that this was a one way trip for Charlie and she wasn't coming back.

The feeling of being watched was ever present, only stronger now. She shrugged off her rucksack and opened a side pocket for one of the torches.

The glass of the lens was broken.

"Fuck! You stupid sod, Charlie!" she hissed to herself. She'd landed on that torch when she threw herself to the ground. She left it in the pocket where it was for now and opened the other side pocket. That torch was intact. She opened the main part of the rucksack and rummaged around in the contents. There was a strong acrid smell as she did so. Her heart lurched as she examined the potential damage in a more urgent, fevered manner. Relief washed over her as she saw there was no noticeable damage and it wasn't a leak that had caused the smell.

She closed the main part of the rucksack up and ensured everything was secure. Lifting the broken torch out she picked the remaining broken glass out of the plastic casing and dropped it in the side pocket with the rest of the broken lens. Then she pushed the slide switch forward. The torch lit up. Good! A small victory! It still worked. She'd take that.

Putting both straps through her arms she stepped into the mouth of The Pipe. The yellow beam of her torch cut a feeble path through the intense darkness. Something about the quality of the light highlighted its temporary existence in The Pipe. The darkness swam around the edge of the torchlight looking for ways to push back in. The darkness was alive and it was angry at this intrusion.

Charlie walked carefully along The Pipe. Pushing against the broiling darkness. The air down here had weight and in that weight was the stench of death. Charlie had missed a trick. She should have brought a mask. The smell was cloying and choked her as she made her way deeper inside The Pipe. Her eyes swam as it intensified. She could not recall it being this bad. But then it had been a long time ago and perhaps when the three of them had intruded that first time the killing had only just begun.

The walk to the gate seemed timeless. Charlie could have walked for a matter of mere minutes or hours. The gate itself looked bigger, more substantial. Coated in rust, but huge and unbreachable it filled The Pipe. Charlie thought back to that time twenty years ago. The gate then was just the right size for a ten year old. Now, it was the right size for the adult her. That should not have been possible, but she knew that it was.

This was the true border between the outside world and the lair of the Bad Man. Once Charlie passed through the gate she was in enemy territory and there really was no going back. Not that she'd ever, truly had the option to go back.

The gate itself stood wide open. This was as Charlie had expected. They had left it open all that time ago and allowed the Bad Man his freedom. She stood at the threshold looking in. The light from her torch marked the borders dissected by the gateway, the beam dimmed halfway along its length at the point it passed over the border. She played the beam of the torch back and forth, seeing it strengthen as she pointed it completely within this side of The Pipe. Watching the change as the beam passed over the border.

Once again she noticed the transition of stone blocks to the solid rock of a cave and the intensifying carvings of misbegotten images on the walls. They had been sporadic at first, infilling more and more as she walked deeper into The Pipe. At the gate, the walls, floor and ceiling were awash with images. Something caught her eye as she moved the torch this way and that. She froze as she focused in on the movement.

It was blood. On the other side of the wall, the carvings were filling with blood. The blood did not pass beyond the gateway. But as she watched in morbid fascination the blood pumped along the grooves and gouges in the rock faces on the other side of the gate. Pumping and pulsing the blood oozed forth. The blood from sacrifices to the Bad Man.

Charlie closed her eyes and composed herself as best she could. She sighed and shrugged, stepping carefully through and over the base of the gate. Her lead foot slipping in the bloody slime on the floor. She could feel droplets from the cave ceiling above her. Could hear them further along The Pipe. Knew this was all for her. Designed by the Bad Man to unhinge her and make his work easier. She grit her teeth, he would not win that easily.

She once more shrugged the pack of her bag and shone the torch into the main compartment as she opened it. Here, by the gate she lightened the load. She would not need to bring the bag with her, so she was leaving it here. She stood and reached for the open gate. Closing a hand around it she pulled.

"Arrggghh!" she cried out as something dug deep into her hand. There had been nothing about her first contact with the gate that had promised this injury. Cradling her bloody hand, she shone the torch on it. The cut was deep and went right across her palm. First blood to the Bad Man.

The pain focused her and made her more determined. All of this had just got real. They were playing for keeps. Charlie knelt again, pulled an old t-shirt from the bottom of her bag, tore some off and wrapped it in her hand. She emptied the rest of her bag. Pocketing the spare torch and a couple of other items. She got up, rounded the gate and placed the padded rucksack against the gate and shouldered it. At first it did not budge. So she stepped back and shone the torch at the hinges.

In the dark, she grinned maniacally. Slipping carefully along the gate she stood at the three hinges. Pulling the fabric from her palm she squeezed her hand over first one hinge, then the next and the next. Lubricating them with her blood. She muttered obscenities at the Bad Man to dispel the pain. Continued grinning; the Bad Man had given her this option. He'd made a mistake.

Back at the other end of the gate, she braced her shoulder against her rucksack. Feet almost on the wall. She pushed. There was a scream of rust on rust and then the gate gave grudgingly. Charlie rocked back and to, pushing and pushing again. The gate gave bit by bit. Fighting all the way. Once it had given though, it was always going to shut.

The catch slid across surprisingly easily.

Charlie's worry was that it would slide open again all too easily. She could not let that happen.

She took her time here. Reminding herself that she would do things her way and in her own time. Now that she had the gate shut they were contained. In the same space. Yes, she was trapped. But so too was the Bad Man and his twisted companion.

Charlie was gambling. All of this was a gamble. It was all she had was a chance and the hope that she would succeed. Part of her gamble was that the Bad Man was weak, that he needed his companion even with the gate

21

open. That The Pipe was the Bad Man's source of power and he could not travel far from The Pipe. He needed his companion and Charlie had a score or two to settle with that fucker.

"I'm coming for you," Charlie whispered to herself as she made ready to leave the gate.

22

Charlie was also banking on her memory of her one and only time in The Pipe. As she remembered it, The Pipe had had a gradual curve that seemed to tighten as they approached the end. The memories of that day were indelible, but she also knew how unreliable memories could be and how memories themselves could have unknown twists and turns.

She exhaled a long breath as The Pipe did indeed begin to curve around. Before coming fully around the corner to journey's end she dropped an item she'd carried with her from the gate. Like the bag, she wouldn't need it any longer. There wasn't much she needed right now other than resolve. She would see this through to the bitter end.

The torch dimmed as she stepped towards the end of The Pipe. She tapped it automatically as though it were faulty. It wasn't. This was the dominion of the dark, and light had no place here. The stench in this place was unholy. Charlie was struggling even before she raised her torch and pointed it at the grotesque tableau before her. Her gorge rising and her stomach rolling. She could not begin to comprehend what she was seeing, only that it had no place in this world. There were parts of living creatures protruding from a mass of flesh and offal. The parts she recognised made it all the more terrible. She avoided the centre piece, knowing from the polaroid she had received at the hotel that this was Archie. There were other human heads. Other people had been sacrificed.

Charlie doubled over, clutching onto her torch as her body convulsed. She vomited violently. Her entire body retching, her guts feeling like they were being punched by the heavy weight champion of the world.

22

"Charlie?" she heard a whisper as the vomiting subsided and she regained control of her body. She turned around slowly, her feet slipping on the wet cave floor. Careful not to look down at what she was standing in. It was more than a smear, her feet were in an obscene sludge that was even now seeping into her trainers. Telling herself not to think about that what it was that she could feel oozing into her trainers and touching her bare skin, and failing badly in that respect.

Her torch fell upon a hooded figure tied to a simple metal and plastic chair. The figure was slumped and unmoving. Kabir must be weakened by his injuries, she needed to free him if he were to stand a chance. She slipped in the slime of putrefaction as she went to him, but managed to keep her feet. She loosed her grip on the torch and caught hold of the back of the chair, the torch landed in the sludge, the heavy battery end sinking in it so the beam lit up part of the wall of death. Thankfully, it gave Charlie enough light to see Kabir by. She fumbled in her pocket, finding a penknife. She opened it then crouched and sawed at the bonds of his left hand. The rope fell away. His hand was free!

"Come on, Kabir!" she hissed as she sawed the knife to and fro on the rope binding his right hand. He did not move. Was she too late? She didn't think so. She sensed his warmth and that he was breathing. She was not too late.

This rope seemed stronger somehow, she may as well be trying to cut it with the pad of her finger, "Come on!" she urged the knife as she redoubled her efforts. Once the knife got a purchase and went through the first of the rope she would get through the rest no problem at all. She was moments away from freeing her friend. She'd thought him dead or as good as. Had thought the Bad Man was using him as bait and would kill him in front of her, enjoying the moment with her as his audience.

A sound behind her. She glanced at the wall of putrid flesh and offal. The sound had come from that direction.

Was it him?

She was panicking now. Struggling for breath. Her movements awkward. Still the knife would not cut through the fucking rope.

She froze.

The sound grew. It was wet and terrible. Without turning to look, she knew that part of the wall of flesh was moving. Something was directly behind her and she was done for. She would be undone if she cast her eyes on whatever terrible monstrosity was emerging from the pile of decaying dead.

"You came," stated a familiar voice.

Charlie's mind reeled. What had she been expecting? A deep gravelly, demonic voice? She looked up at the body on the chair. The person she was trying to free was fully clothed. The clothing was nondescript; jeans and a long sleeved top.

The photo of Kabir. He had been bare chested, hadn't he? And the hood could conceal the face of anyone. She hadn't dared lift it because Kabir had been missing an eye and she couldn't bear to see his ruined face. She felt responsible for that. She felt responsible for it all.

The person sitting in front of her was not Kabir.

"Stand up, Charlie. It's me!" said Kabir from behind her. His voice did not belong in this place, not like this. He sounded cheerful. Happy even. A powerful torch beam flicked on, illuminating the space more effectively than her torch was managing to. "I brought a better torch this time, Charlie. And with yours, I now have a spare!"

What kind of a trick was this? Charlie pushed herself to standing and turned around slowly.

"Spare?" Charlie croaked as she forced the words out. Unable to process what was going on. Kabir was stood in front of her. His chest was bare, but he looked unharmed, "Your eye?" asked Charlie, not understanding.

Kabir chuckled, "oh that!? That was make up. Amazing what you can buy on the internet! I would show you. It's in my pocket, but…" he shrugged and raised both hands. In his left hand he held the large torch. In the other he held a sharp, wicked looking knife. It looked like a butcher's knife. Charlie supposed that it was.

"What's going on, Kabir?" the quality of Charlie's voice had changed. She was no longer conveying confusion as much as sadness and disappointment. Perhaps even resignation in the recognition that there is nothing more evil than man himself.

"Bit slow on the uptake aren't we, Charlie?" Kabir smirked at her.

Charlie wanted to wipe the smirk from his face, "You're behind all of this?"

"Well, not exactly..." Kabir shrugged.

"Not exactly?" Charlie blew out a deep breath, unable to comprehend why Kabir would do this, "do you even know what you're dealing with here?"

Kabir smirked again, "Yeah, her." He gestured towards the figure on the chair with the knife as he said this dismissively.

"Her?" Charlie turned to look at the woman on the chair, "It was a woman doing all of this?"

"Not all of it Charlie," Kabir corrected. Sounding proud of his part in all of whatever this was.

"But *why?!*" Charlie really couldn't get it.

"Lift the hood Charlie, tell me what you see," Kabir nodded at the slumped figure.

Charlie did as she was told. Curious at what she would reveal. The hood wasn't tied, so she lifted it carefully away, found that she had stopped breathing as she waited for the face. To see it. To understand it.

Kabir watched Charlie, noted the lack of recognition on her face. Not even a flicker, "Do you recognise her, Charlie?"

Charlie shook her head. The woman sitting slumped on the chair was a similar age to her and Kabir, that checked out with what she had been expecting, but she'd also thought she'd recognise the person who was doing all of this, only now realising that her hope was that by seeing the face of the killer she would understand, that all of the pieces would fall into place and she'd know the *why* of it.

The woman's face was badly bruised and she was unconscious, her breathing arhythmic, "You hit her?" it was more a statement than a question.

"She didn't seem to want to go along with my plan," Kabir smirked his smirk again.

"Who is she?"

"Karen Green," Kabir told her, "ring a bell?"

Charlie shook her head, she didn't recognise the woman, doubted she'd remember the child she had been and the name was not at all familiar.

"That's part of the problem right there," explained Kabir, "Karen here felt aggrieved that we three were popular and yet she went unnoticed. She's one of those faces you see. She's background. Never to be noticed. Unremarkable. And that really pissed her off."

Kabir paused and laughed.

"What?" said Charlie, wondering what was so funny.

"Then again, she was already pissed off thanks to her weirdo Mum..."

"What do you mean, Kabir?"

"Oh, her Mum was a right old nutter! Did a number on old Karen here, didn't she Kazzer?"

Kabir was talking to the prone and unconscious figure on the chair and didn't expecting a reply. He went on, "Does the name Keiron ring a bell at all, Charlie?"

Charlie's breath caught in her throat, "Keiron Green?"

"That's the one! You remember *him* don't you!?"

"Him? That was Karen?"

"Yeah, her Mum wanted a boy. So when Karen made for a difficult birth and did enough damage to prevent her Mum fulfilling that particular dream? Well, Mother got creative. Karen could be that boy. So that's what she did. She brought Karen up as Keiron and fucked with her head In the process!"

Kabir chuckled again, "she resented us lot all the more for that. Us with our normal lives and friendships and her with her mentalist Mum making her pretend to be a boy, only she didn't even know she was pretending until she was about... oh, ten years old?"

"So she decided to kill us?" Charlie asked quietly.

"Pretty much yeah, well she'd got a taste for it, as you can see from this little lot here and as we saw when we invaded her *special place*. She'd been killing animals for years. Started by hurting her Mum's cat and she got a kick from that, so..." Kabir nodded at the wall of putrefying remains behind him.

"Why wait for twenty years though?" asked Charlie still wanting to know the *why* of it. Why had this all started up again now?

22

"Ah! I had wondered that too! Karen's Mum moved to look after her Gran. Lives down Bournemouth way, and it turned out that Karen's Gran was a limpet when it came to clinging onto life. So they ended up in Bournemouth until a few months ago. Karen's Gran died three years back and Karen's Mum took her place. Fell ill as the old bird died, lumbering poor Karen with the duty to care for her. Only Karen didn't give her dear Mother the option to linger or to cling, she peeled her fingers away from life and carried on peeling..."

Kabir moved to one side and pointed his torch beam at a mess of skin and muscle, "that's her there. Karen had hung up her killing knife for twenty years and then she cut her teeth on her own Mum. Heart warming story isn't it, Charlie."

Charlie didn't like the way Kabir said her name. It was ridiculous in the circumstances, she knew, but Kabir said it like she was dirt. Dirt that he could no longer stomach and intended doing something about.

"So she didn't kill for twenty years?"

"No, she tried to explain that to me. She went really weird. Kept talking about this place and *him*. Whoever *him* is. At first I thought she had an accomplice and she confused matters by saying he was much more than that. Her master and all this mumbo jumbo about reclaiming the Seven Sisters and a Reign of Darkness. Off her rocker, but what do you expect from a psycho killer?" Kabir shrugged again, as though he were talking about the manager of his football team, not the debauched slaughter of innocents.

"So apart from her Mum, she only killed when she was around this place?"

Kabir nodded affirmation, "even then..."

Charlie understood then, "she came here first didn't she?"

"Yeah, said something about the dreams getting stronger and having to come back. After her Mum, erm... passed away, she moved back here and that's when we started to get the polaroids."

"Did she kill Archie?"

Kabir chuckled, "Oh she was so pissed off about that! What a fuck up! She was only just getting started. Planned it for ages. And then Archie dies of a heart attack and screws up all her fun!"

Charlie drew a long breath, trying to hold herself together, "where do you come into this, Kabir?"

"Me?" Kabir grinned, "I saw my opportunity and I took it!"

Charlie screwed her face up, not getting what Kabir meant.

"Come on, Charlie. You're not stupid! I had one half of Archie's house. It's bought and paid for and then there's his money and share portfolio. Archie really was a bit of a whizz. I didn't want to lose half of it to you and that first photo? Someone wanted you dead, so I waited and when that person came, I struck a deal with them. And here you are, just like we planned. Only..."

"You double crossed her," Charlie stated.

"Yup, Karen was so caught up in the prospect of peeling you like the proverbial onion she didn't think things through. There was no way I was going to be her next biology project, so there she is with a bang on the head and tied to the chair. She's a loose end." Again that dismissive tone. Kabir was cold and detached. Made of the stuff Charlie had thought the killer was made of. Why hadn't she seen it before?

Kabir sneered at Charlie, more of a snarl, "You didn't see it coming did you?" he laughed bitterly at her, "of course you didn't! That's the whole point you stupid bitch!"

Kabir was winding himself up, getting his blood up. She could see the rage welling up in him. He was waving the knife, stabbing it towards her to emphasise some of his words.

"You and Archie. Fucking golden girl and fucking golden boy. Always thought you were so special. No wonder Karen hated you with a vengeance. Where was I in your world, eh? I bet you and Archie laughed as you both ignored me and lost touch! Why did you cut me out you bitch!?"

"I..." stammered Charlie, backing away. "I didn't!"

Kabir was having none of it, his spittle flecked lips were drawn back as he stepped towards her. His muscles tought. He was readying himself to kill her. A small part of Charlie. A detached part, wondered if he could do it. It was one thing to think about killing someone, but to actually do it and do it like this, with a knife, up close. There was something intimate about this. Was Kabir really going to go through with this?

22

Charlie did her best to ignore that voice, there was hope in that voice. It wanted to believe that Kabir would step back from the brink and redeem himself. If he didn't then Charlie would present a passive figure and would stand no chance as Kabir thrust the knife into her again and again. She was stepping back slowly and as casually as she possibly could. Trying not to show fear, not wanting to provoke Kabir. She needed those precious seconds to find a move or action that may well save her life or at least buy her some more time.

Movement. Not Kabir. Not a killing blow. The creaking of plastic and metal, and the sound of someone else in The Pipe.

Kabir noticed it. Glanced to his right side. Looked back towards Charlie and took one more step towards her before fully understanding what it was that he had just seen. He glanced again, confirming what his first look had provided him.

Kabir stopped, snarled at Charlie, "Oh you fucking bitch! You freed the psycho! Why the fucking fuck would you *do* that!!?"

Karen was getting up. Getting to her feet and standing. Charlie watched her still bound wrist. She hadn't managed to cut through that with the small pocket knife she'd been using. The pocket knife she'd placed in her hoody pocket, blade still out. Karen levered her arm up from the wrist as she rose and the rope parted as though it were wet spaghetti.

Karen was muttering something as she found her feet. Chanting something over and over and over…

Row, row, row
Row, row, row
Row, row, row
Row, row, row

Then she raised her voice screeching the final words in an awful crescendo…

Don't forget to scream!

Her eyes were wild and filled with madness. Spittle fell from her lips as she yelled the last words.

Kabir turned to face the other woman. Charlie watched them both, they were side on to her now. Standing only a couple of feet apart from each other, looking appraisingly at each other like two dancers considering their prospective partner.

Would you like to dance?

Kabir breathed just the one word, "You…"

In answer, Karen took up the muttering chant again…

Row, row, row

Row, row, row

The tableau changed before Charlie's eyes, because as Karen found her feet and stood erect she did not stop unfurling. Somehow she grew. Taller and bigger. Darker. She loomed over Kabir, more than she had been. All the while, Kabir gazed at Karen's face. Fascinated. Enthralled. His jaw slackened and dropped open. Both of his hands dropped to his sides. He shrank as Karen rose before him. All of his rage and bravado leaked out of him. The hunter was now the prey. A fieldmouse gazing up at the growing shadow and helpless as the claws encircled it.

Row, row, row

Row, row, row

Charlie looked on in surprise and something like awe as Kabir seemed to offer the knife up to Karen. Only it wasn't Karen. It was the Bad Man and it was time for Kabir to honour his part of the deal. To make good on the pre-existing bargain that had never gone away.

Row, row, row

Row, row, row

The knife slipped easily from Kabir's right hand to the Bad Man's left hand. It made a slow and graceful one hundred and eighty degree turn through the space between them and there it paused, pointing at Kabir's crotch. Even in the strange light that had dimmed as Karen had joined the fray, Charlie could see the dark patch on Kabir's joggers. He had wet himself as he stood in the Bad Man's shadow. He had wet himself just as his friend Archie had twenty years previously.

Row, row, row

Row, row, row

22

The next moment was truly awful. The knife, as though it had a mind of its own, flew towards Kabir and kept going even as it sank into his flesh. Kabir gasped as the Bad Man sank the knife to the hilt. They stood like that for a moment, drawn closer by the knife. Then the Bad Man's hand worked slowly and languorously up and down. The two of them moved together like lovers. Only the Bad Man was playing with the hilt of his knife and working it slowly to and fro and as he did, it made its way upwards. The Bad Man worked the knife slowly but surely up towards Kabir's throat. Taking his time.

Row, row, row

Row, row, row

Too late, Kabir brought his hands up as though to stop his undoing, in vain, he attempted to hold himself together, eyes wide and uncomprehending. He slipped to his knees in the rotten grime and looked up at the Bad Man as though praying to him, his guts spilled out in front of him. He looked down at them, then keeled forward into the mess. Twitching like a landed fish as he died.

23

Charlie felt an eerie sense of calm as she looked on at her former friend being slaughtered. It didn't help to think of him as he was in his last moments; a cold betrayer intent on ending her. What she saw was the Kabir of her childhood. Her friend and companion. And now he was fallen. The Bad Man had ended him.

She pushed her hands deeper in her pockets and enclosed her fingers around objects in each. Then she waited for the Bad Man to turn towards her. She was next and her odds had only momentarily improved.

Instead of turning towards her, he crouched over Kabir and buried his face in Kabir's neck. There was a brief struggle underneath the Bad Man, Kabir finding a final reserve of strength, raising his arms and pushing against his attacker. He groaned and his efforts subsided. His leg kicked a few times more. A final moan and all that remained was a wet sucking sound as the Bad Man sucked and drank at the tear in Kabir's throat. Yet again, there was something intimate and sexual about what Charlie was seeing, terrible as it was. She realised the Bad Man had been stroking Kabir throughout and still was. And under the sounds of his feeding were gentle moans of his own mingled with the lighter and higher pitched moans of Karen.

As the feeding ended, Karen seemed to shrink. The darkness left her and it was Karen who stood to face Charlie. Charlie gently opened her fingers and chose a different object in her pocket, she was changing her plan. She hoped she was making the right choice.

Instead of approaching Charlie, Karen reached down under the chair and lifted an old and worn polaroid camera. She pointed it at Kabir's broken and

23

torn body.

CLICK!

WHIR!

The polaroid camera ejected a piece of white card which Karen plucked from it and waved in the air, drying it. She stopped. Looked at the photo and smiled warmly at what she saw, "I think I got his best side!" she said as she pocketed the photo in the back pocket of her jeans. She crouched and placed the polaroid camera back under the chair.

Karen turned back towards Charlie and casually wiped the blood and gore from around her mouth with the back of her sleeve. She smiled at Charlie with what would have been a warm and friendly smile had her teeth not been stained almost black with her friend's blood.

"Where's he gone?" asked Charlie.

"Who? You're friend? Can't you see that the master has taken him?" Karen was playing dumb, her voice trilling and playful as though they were exchanging pleasantries at a social occasion.

"I don't mean, Kabir. You know I don't mean him."

Karen smiled her serene smile, "Your friend was a bad person, Charlie. And the best of it was you didn't know! We did though. We saw right through him. Now you can see right through him too!" Karen pushed Kabir with her foot and he rolled over from his side to flat on his back.

Charlie tried not to look, but couldn't help but be drawn to the sight, there was a horrible wet sound as he fell onto his back. Kabir was wide open for all to see. It was grotesque. That is not Kabir. That is not Kabir. Charlie said over and over inside her own head.

"Oh! But it is!" said Karen gleefully.

Charlie's mouth fell open. Karen had heard her thoughts.

"Oh don't look so shocked! This is my special place! All things are possible here!"

"Because of the Bad Man?" asked Charlie.

Karen giggled, "Is that what you call him? She raised a hand to her mouth in a horrible approximation of coquettishness, "I suppose he can be bad can't he? But then you already know that." She dropped her hand and everything changed. She looked serious, baleful. "I should be angry at you. He's *MINE!*"

Charlie stepped back at the sudden, venomous shout. It had come from nowhere and shocked and surprised her.

Karen cocked her head to one side, playful, her voice soft again, "but I can share. I know it's me he likes best. He'll have his fun with you and then there will only be me and him. That's what counts and that's what we both want…"

Karen had closed the gap between them, raised her free right hand to Charlie's hair, playing with a strand.

"F..f..fun?" Charlie stammered.

"Of course," Karen slipped her fingers through Charlie's hair and stroking the back of her neck, drawing closer. Charlie could feel Karen's breath on her. It was unnatural. It smelt foul. Of death.

"You killed Billy, didn't you?" Charlie tried to keep her voice level and calm, didn't want to betray her anger and fear. She was aware of the knife in Karen's other hand and how easily she could drive it into Charlie and end her there and then.

Despite this, a cloud passed over Karen's face, "yes, that was a mistake. I was clumsy and it went wrong. He was going to be my first…"

Charlie bit her lip, it was as she thought. Thankfully no worse than she had thought. Billy, like Archie had escaped Karen and the Bad Man. Escaped their worst intentions.

Karen's face lit up, "we all make mistakes, don't we? I've made amends to the master since. He was so pleased when I came back. And of course there was your Dad, Charlie. The master taught me there were many ways you could kill someone. Your Dad was different. We haunted him and we broke him. The master opened him up in a way that a knife doesn't, but it's just as beautiful. And satisfying. The master introduced me to pleasure that most mortals can never even dream of. And you'll understand soon enough."

Karen drew even closer and as Charlie tried to subtly mirror the movement and ease away keeping the distance between them, her shoulders touched the wall of The Pipe behind her. She was struggling to keep a lid on her revulsion and the anger she held towards Karen. Right now, it was scant consolation to hear that her Dad hadn't killed himself, that this was all the work of this twisted bitch and the Bad Man.

Karen leaned in and brushed her lips against Charlie's neck. Charlie shuddered at the unexpected touch. Karen mistook this as an encouraging response, "yes, that's it," she whispered in Charlie's ear.

Charlie shuddered again and much to her horror wondered if she were responding. They said there was only a fine line between sex and death and right now her body was alive, senses heightened as adrenaline coursed through her. She was wondering whether she should play along only to find that she already was, her indecision and reluctance to anger Karen or provoke a sudden, deadly move was all the answer Karen needed.

Charlie went with it, telling herself that she wasn't, that she couldn't. That she was filled with revulsion, rage and hatred for this person and this place.

"So, where is the master now?" Charlie said softly. As she spoke, she noticed that she'd tilted her head slightly away from Karen, but this had exposed her neck invitingly.

Karen sighed and kissed Charlie's neck, "oh the master is resting. He needs a lot of rest. He has fed though, so I don't think we have long. He gives me time with our play things and toys. I had a lot more time with your friend there. It's true what they say about men, you know."

"And what do they say?" asked Charlie, shifting under Karen, disguising the movement with a sigh.

"Well, they only think with their cocks sometimes, don't they? And if you're a very good girl, then that's all they can think with. Doesn't take much to lead them and bend them to your will."

"Did the master teach you that too?" Charlie freed her hands from their pockets, where they had been slightly pinned by Karen's weight, she slipped her left hand around Karen's waist.

"You know he did," Karen planted a string of kisses along Charlie's neck and nibbled her earlobe, moaning against her. Charlie's back arched involuntarily. She was doing her best to hold herself back, but that was counterproductive. And Karen was making her think back to the hotel bath and the Bad Man slipping into her thoughts and then into her as she held back then to build her pleasure. Part of her wanted to give herself over to this. It was wrong and it was unexpected, but she was responding and it was buying her time and…

No! She couldn't. She had to do something and right now. The longer she allowed Karen to play with her the more her chances slipped away, the more her resolve would slip away. Karen was softening her up and making her compliant. Charlie could feel the fight leaving her.

"I didn't need the master when it came to Kabir, he was all too willing and I knew exactly which buttons to press. He was putty in my hands. Well, not… " Karen was warming to her subject. Her mouth more insistent. Her tongue lapping. Teeth nipping. She was moving rhythmically against Charlie now.

"Karen?" something about Charlie's voice. Commanding. Demanding attention.

Karen lifted her head away from Charlie's neck looked at her, her face forming a question that Charlie now answered, "Shut up!"

Karen did not notice Charlie's free hand as it came up in an arc. But she did feel a dull thud as Charlie's fist clubbed her left ear.

"What?" Karen said, her face now a picture of shock as she stumbled back two steps. Her knife forgotten, fingers of her left hand opening and coming up to cup her ear where there was a terrible roaring like crashing waves and a strange numbness. Her fingers scrabbled around what she found there. Comprehension taking some time to come. Something hard was protruding from her ear. Something was in her ear. No, in her head. Her body canted to the left, as though the weight of the object sticking out of her ear was weighing it down. Her left hand came away from her ear and she waved it towards Charlie as though showing her the blood and goo on her fingers and palm.

"You b…b…b…" Karen's words faded away and she formed a large O with her mouth; a fish dying in the air.

She stumbled sideways, slipping and almost falling. She had not seen Charlie stoop to lift her knife from the slime beneath her. What she did see was Charlie step forward and close the distance between them.

"Now where were we?" Charlie slipped her left arm back around Karen's

23

waist and resumed their embrace.

Karen's eyes, confused, yet hopeful. Charlie wouldn't embrace her if... this was all a mistake, surely... this wasn't supposed to happen... master? Where was the master? Her master.

And then Karen's eyes went wide as her body stiffened against Charlie's, and she knew. She knew and then was gone, her eyes dimming, glazing over, the light of life leaving her.

Charlie didn't think to withdraw the knife from the back of Karen's head as Karen slumped against her. Instead Charlie stepped away from the dead weight and let her fall face first into the slime of the floor, her killing knife protruding from her neck, the blade deep in her head.

24

Charlie hadn't come back to The Pipe expecting answers, not really. She was always going to ask the questions, but she knew that life had a habit of not giving you what you thought you wanted. But it might sometimes give you what you needed, you had to be wise enough to see this when it happened and grateful too.

Charlie had got some of her questions answered and not with the sort of answers that were bigger questions all of their own. She was up on the deal and for that she was grateful. And now she had evened the odds. It was one on one and from what Karen had told her, the Bad Man was not at the height of his powers. He had needed Karen. The killing had stopped when she had left Dinsdale. Karen hadn't killed for twenty years and Charlie was reasonably certain that the Bad Man had not found another companion to take her place. Even with the gate wide open and the Bad Man given more freedom, the power of the Seven Sisters had held him back and kept him in a weakened state.

She had to end this now though. She had to right the wrongs of twenty years ago, because the Bad Man had waited a long time. He could wait. And when an opportunity came along, he would take it. Kabir was proof of that. Kabir had been greedy. His head had been turned by the money, then Karen had seduced him and made him promises and played him. Once he was in The Pipe he was the Bad Man's plaything and Karen had gone along with the role play until it was her moment to do what she was always going to do; kill Kabir.

Kabir had unwittingly helped Charlie. He was a random factor and however much the Bad Man could control people, there was always a force of will and the potential for something unexpected to happen. The Bad Man had experienced this with the seventh sister of a seventh sister and it seemed that he didn't learn, or perhaps he did, but this was how he worked and he had no other way of being. That he was the ultimate bully. If he cowed his victims and they did not stand up to him then he won. But if someone were to stand and face him then there was a chance that things wouldn't all go the Bad Man's way. Charlie hoped she'd read this right and that she would get that chance that she needed.

* * *

Charlie stepped over the prone body of Karen, a sudden paranoia clutching at her as she was astride the body. What if Karen was not dead. Charlie was vulnerable and...

In her mind's eye a hand shot out and grabbed her ankle, it clamped her leg like a vice and squeezed. Charlie's cry of pain was choked in her throat as the hand twisted viciously and she heard a loud crack as her ankle broke. The force and violence of it threw her sideways into the mass of decaying flesh and offal. Her head was submerged in gore and she began to suffocate. Someone stepped behind her. Arms grabbed her and held her there and however much she flailed and struggled, all she succeeded in doing was pushing further into the putrefied gore. Her mouth opened in an attempt to draw a breath and it filled with a vile liquid. She was drowning in death...

Charlie shook her head, "No!" she cried and with a force of will she pushed the images away. The Bad Man had somehow got inside her head and had used those images to confuse her, or worse. She stepped over the body and picked up Kabir's torch. Cautiously stepping back over Karen's body, she went to the chair and moved it back a yard.

Her eyes fell upon the polaroid camera which had been exposed as she moved the chair. The sight of it filled her with a wave of revulsion. Those fucking polaroids! She lifted her foot and stamped down on the camera. There was a cracking sound, but the camera didn't give.

STAMP!

STAMP!

STAMP!

She smashed down with her foot again and again, but the camera stubbornly held together. It would not smash into a thousand pieces.

CLICK!

WHIR!

Somehow, Charlie had caught the button and taken a fucking photo! She aimed a kick at the thing and punted it as hard as she could, it hit the wall of The Pipe half way up and there was now a satisfying crash as it broke, it ricocheted off the wall at an angle and skittered back down the tunnel of The Pipe.

Charlie stood there gasping, out of breath. She'd given her all and laid into that camera. She did her best to calm herself and regain some composure, then she placed the torch next to the chair on the ground so it illuminated the wall of dead bodies. That was where he was. That was the Bad Man's lair.

She sat. Facing that wall.

Now she reached into the pockets of her hoody, her fingers finding the objects she had been after previously. The two items other than the penknife that she had brought with her for this moment. She was pleased to feel the item in her right pocket was still intact. She brought it out and put one end in her mouth. Even with the stench of The Pipe, she caught a reassuring aroma of tobacco.

In her other hand she brought out a zippo lighter and flicked it open. She lit the cigar, drawing on it until it was properly lit. She choked slightly as she drew the smoke through the cigar. She wasn't used to smoking. Cigars were her Dad's thing. She remembered sitting with him in the back garden of their house as he smoked a huge cigar. It was his Christmas tradition, but Mum hated the smell and banished him outside when he smoked. As she got older, he'd let her hold the flame to light it. Told her that you didn't inhale

24

the smoke like you did with a cigarette. That it was a much more leisurely pursuit. A small piece of luxury and celebration.

She drew on the cigar, tasting it. Smelling it. Savouring the sensations and enjoying them all the more as they provided some respite from the stench of this place.

Now she would wait.

Charlie waited for the Bad Man.

She didn't know how long she waited. Only that she was half way through her cigar and the light from the small, discarded and forgotten torch guttered and went out a short while before the Bad Man's arrival.

Several times, Charlie's gaze fell upon the knife sticking up from the Bad Man's companion, Karen. She considered it. Should she go over there and take it. It couldn't hurt to have it could it? Feel the reassuring heft of a weapon?

No, the knife was useless against the Bad Man and should Charlie go over there and attempt to retrieve it all she would be doing was showing her weakness and she would blunt her focus. The Bad Man could even be watching and waiting for her to do this. In the act of withdrawing the knife, Charlie would summon the Bad Man. Was it worth pulling the knife for that reason alone? Charlie thought not. That the timing of the Bad Man's arrival would then put Charlie on the back foot.

In her consideration of the knife, her weight had lifted from the chair. Twice. She had almost acted. The will to act was powerful. To do something. To be the master of her own destiny. Waiting was hard. It took a force of will. Charlie was ready. She needed to remain focused and ready. Timing was everything. She had had the time to prepare and seat herself in anticipation of the Bad Man's arrival.

He would come.

They both knew that.

It was as she finally dismissed thoughts of taking the knife and dug in awaiting the Bad Man's arrival that the second torch, the torch she had brought to The Pipe, went out. The shock of it took Charlie's breath away. The flickering and guttering caused movements in The Pipe before her. The wall of flesh and decay seemed to pulse and move as though it were coming alive. This drew Charlie's attention like never before, she had looked away as much as she could and even when her eyes were upon the mass of dead flesh that filled The Pipe and blocked it up, she looked without seeing.

The wall looked like it was breathing as the second torch's beam flickered on and off. It seemed as though it moved closer to Charlie with every breath. Charlie saw the animals writhing within the wall at first and then the people. There were more people in the wall than Karen's mother and Archie. She could see parts of others as she looked on in fascinated terror, mesmerised by the grotesque flesh as it threatened to fully awaken and reach out and take her.

The torch went out. The Pipe was that bit darker for it and Charlie lamented the loss of light. It underlined her solitude. She was alone in The Pipe with the Bad Man and no one knew she was here. No one would ever think to look for her here, even with her car parked near Dinsdale Woods, but that was the way it had to be.

As Charlie's eyes adjusted to the change in light, she could have sworn that the light from her torch had also dimmed. It was the dark though, it was growing and gathering around her. And now the pulsing and movement was all around her. Like a dark heartbeat. And now it encased her narrowing The Pipe even further and highlighting all the more the awful scene before her. Death and the promise of death. There was an inevitability about it that weighed heavily upon Charlie.

She was about to draw on the cigar again when she noticed that she could see her breath. The air in The Pipe was colder now. She pulled on the cigar, drawing some comfort from the glow at its end and the act of smoking it. Her eyes had never left the wall though and now she saw that even with the second torch now lying dead on the floor, the wall had not stop moving. The movement seemed to be localised at the very centre. The wall pushed outwards and then returned. Outwards and returned. Outwards and returned. The movement mirrored the pulsing of the darkness around Charlie and it had a hypnotic, almost soporific effect on her.

Then she saw what it was that was moving. It was Archie. As Charlie

24

looked toward her dead friend and as she focused upon him, his dead eyelids shot open, he fixed her with a lifeless glare and opened his mouth. No words came forth, but his meaning was clear as his hand emerged from the filth around him and he pointed at her.

You did this!
You did this!
This is on you!
This is ALL YOUR FAULT!

It was. Charlie had always known that. She had carried the guilt with her for twenty years. She was the one of the three who had the final say. Oh! Archie liked to think he ruled the roost and most of the time he did, but Kabir was his equal and a force to be reckoned with providing some of the checks and balances, it was Charlie though who had the power of veto. It was Charlie who really lead the group. They all three of them knew that really. Archie was the figurehead, but it was Charlie who made the big decisions and so it was her… She had allowed them to venture forth into hell itself. Put the three of them in mortal danger and worse still, compounded all of this by leaving that gate wide open. Open so that the Bad Man could follow them and pick them off one by one. First though, he had come for Charlie's brother and her Dad. The Bad Man had always known that it was her who had led the three into his lair and he had left her until last so he could exact his terrible retribution.

Charlie knew it was more than that though. Had known even before she had come here. Known before she had heard the whispered words of the seventh sister of a seventh sister. The Bad Man feared her. She was a woman. He hated women. He hated all women, but the worst of those women were the women who were at the height of their sexual powers. And Charlie had been untouched by a man which heightened her particular powers even further. She wasn't a seventh sister of a seventh sister, but she was all there was and she was enough. That was what the seventh sister had told her. She was a match for this evil. More than a match.

Stand strong and never falter in the face of evil and you will prevail, Charlie.

The ancient sister had given her one more piece of advice.

THE PIPE

Focus on your love and never let go.

That was what she had been doing ever since she'd left the clearing. Mostly, she had been picturing Billy her sweet little brother. Forever young. But she thought of all the people she had loved. That love never went away and it would not be denied. She thought of her friends and the times they had spent together. That special summer where The Sun had chosen to take a long holiday over their town and look over them day after day. Painting the world with her light and filling them with it. With joy. With the joy that only a ten year old exploring the world and using their little bit of independence could feel. A special and pure joy that would stand out as a beacon in their lives; everything is possible, you are beautiful, as is the world around you, never forget this and never forget the way you felt in this moment.

That is why Charlie smiled as the wall of putrid flesh moved and partially collapsed and the Bad Man stepped forth to confront her. To take her life and feast upon her. To take her totally in the most terrible way imaginable. She smiled, nodded and drew upon her cigar.

It was time.

The Bad Man stood before Charlie. He was not so much a man as man shaped. He was darkness. A manifestation of darkness. The darkness that formed this creature was so concentrated, so intense it formed an abyss, to look upon him for too long would see a person lost forever. Lost forever within that darkness. An eternity of evil.

Charlie stood and looked upon her adversary. And what she saw was not so terrible. It just *was*. It could not be denied.

There was a moment betwixt the two of them. And in that moment the Bad Man hesitated. There was something in his demeanour that said he lost the absolute certainty which was his trademark. Was it a slither of recognition? He certainly saw something that made him pause. It wasn't that his minion had been slain, he had not deigned to look upon her fallen form. She was gone. She had fulfilled her purpose for a time and that was that. He would waste no time upon her. It was that this was not in the script. This was not how it went as he stepped forth to take a human life. This human was not like the others.

24

This one shone.

She was dangerous.

Did she remind him of another?

If she did, he dismissed the memory and with it all thoughts of what this woman may or may now be. All that mattered was the here and now and that this woman had transgressed, that she was here in front of him and she must be punished.

He did not speak. He brought with him utter silence. It was ominous and frightful. He stood before Charlie, filling The Pipe and promising oblivion. His very presence broke a person's will, and yet…

Charlie stepped towards the Bad Man and spoke.

"You came," she said warmly, as though they were two lovers meeting for a tryst.

The Dark Man stood motionless. What was this woman doing? She could not prevent the inevitable. She was going to die and anything she did could only make her ending worse. He would make her pay for her insolence. Draw out her death so she felt every cut, gouge and bite. He would fill her with fire and then fill her with ice. He would undo her and then allow her back from the very brink, to cling on to hope before he started in on her again and again and again. He could prolong her agonies for what would seem like an eternity.

YOU CANNOT DENY ME

The Dark Man had spoken. The voice did not come from a mouth. It came from The Pipe itself and filled it. Charlie heard it inside herself more than without.

"Oh, but I can," whispered Charlie and she stepped closer, slipping an arm around her nemesis.

NO!

The Dark Man saw a glimpse of Charlie's purpose, but it was too late. With her free hand, she threw the cigar behind her. It lay there for a moment, a red glow in the darkness of The Pipe. A tiny dot which would soon be consumed by the cold and damp and darkness. An insignificance.

Yet the Dark Man watched it and as he did, a flame sprang forth from where the cigar lay. A flame which grew brighter and larger and continued growing upwards until it broke away from where the Dark Man and Charlie stood and raced away and around the corner...

NO!

The Dark Man cried furiously. Charlie felt The Pipe shake with his anger. Took the opportunity to wrap her other arm around him, now that it had done its job with the cigar. She hadn't turned. Knew from the Dark Man's reaction that she had thrown true. Heard the wumph! As the petrol caught.

She gave herself a moment to think about that fire, hoped that it had caught that fucking camera in its embrace and was melting it, burning it. Ending it completely.

Charlie had come prepared. She'd brought fire and she'd brought metal. Right now, the line of burning petrol was heading back to the gate. At the gate it would ignite a concoction of petrol, vegetable oil and a few other ingredients she had found to hand to increase the temperature it would burn at. She'd packed the bolt of the gate and it's housing with metal and encased it in wadding and rags soaked in the accelerant. The gate would be welded shut.

There was more. Charlie didn't think that this alone would hold the Bad Man. His imprisonment required more.

Her.

Charlie had to hold the Dark Man back while the fire did its work. She had to stop him entirely and there was only one way to do that. She had to seal the Dark Man in.

She tightened her embrace.

The Dark Man felt her arms enfold him and realised the significance of what she was doing.

WHAT? NO!

He shrugged her off. Only, he didn't. What should have been easy was not. He moved more forcefully, but there was no give. What was this? This was not possible! She was a mere woman and this was his dominion. Here especially, he was too powerful for her. She was his play thing and his sustenance. And yet...

24

GRRAAAAAH!

The roar preceded an even greater effort from the Dark Man to stop this madness. To strike Charlie down and put out that fire. Did she really think she could do this?

No.

She believed.

He had to stop her. He pressed his fingers to her sides and pushed. Tendrils of ice pierced her flesh, impaling her. He pushed forth. This would end. Now.

Charlie looked up at the Dark Man. Her face a picture of serenity. It glowed. And as the Dark Man peered down at this strange sight, the light grew out from Charlie filling the tunnel and diminishing the Dark Man.

YOU...

The Dark Man said it quietly, almost reverently.

Then the lights went out and The Pipe was returned to utter darkness.

Epilogue

The next Summer is a scorcher.

The adults talk about the hot, lazy summers of their childhood and how there hadn't been one like this since. Their children pay little heed to the reminiscences of their parents. Lazy? Now is the time to play! They are solar powered machines and the long Summer days give them more energy than they have ever had. Their parents watch them venture forth into that magical sunlight and envy them their youth and energy.

Let them make their memories. Those memories will see them through the rest of their lives.

The Sun looks down upon Dinsdale, the place that was once, not so long ago, as far as The Sun is concerned, known as Seven Sisters. She watches these creatures of the light and smiles upon them. The young ones are a delight. She wonders at how so many of them grow weary of life and the light she provides them as their years pass. What is it that makes them avoid her and live out their days in the darkness. Some will embrace her light in their final years, if they make it that far. It's a big gamble to wait that long. The Sun knows this; tomorrow is never a certainty. These humans close their eyes and go into the darkness every night never knowing whether they will open them again to see the light of another day. The Sun is rebirth and the herald to another day of life.

The Sun watches as three friends ride their bikes down from their housing estate to the woodland. The Sun has a particular soft spot for these woods. They are special, but then trees always are. Trees are a part of the seasons and the circle of life.

The three children ride into the woods in a row. The Sun sees them through the dappling leaves, peddling away as though their lives depended

EPILOGUE

upon it. They reach a clearing and drop their bikes in the long grass. They are laughing. Laughing at nothing in particular, as children have a wont to do. Laughter is a part of their living, an expression of their joy as they play. They run around in circles, chasing each other and pretending to be whatever they want to be on this particular day in this particular moment. One of them stops suddenly and pushes another roughly to the floor. There is intent there. He meant it. The fallen child pays no heed to that intent though. This is her friend and that is all that counts. She sees the best in him, she sees his light shining through, even as he is bundled over by the third of the friends. This one, the girl who sees the best in people, is the glue that will see these three remain friends through thick and thin. Best friends forever.

The child reminds The Sun of another little girl. A girl who not only saw the best in everything, but did her best too. As The Sun thinks of her, she gazes upon a spot further into the woods. A space in the densest part of the woods which opens out ever so slightly.

The Sun shines upon a sapling oak which has found a way out through a pile of old, broken bricks. The bricks once formed part of an ancient tunnel which over time seems to have collapsed in on itself. It's a strange place for a tree to choose to start out its life, but as The Sun knows, life finds a way.

In time, this tree will grow to be one of the largest and tallest trees in these woods. It will push through those bricks and eventually dwarf them and it will stand sentry at the entrance to the fallen tunnel. And it will bring light and life to this part of the woods. That is already happening, The Sun can see the seeds of the transformation.

Soon, as far as The Sun is concerned anyway, Charlie will join her Seven Sisters. The seven large oak trees who encircle her and watch over her and stand guard over an ancient evil which Charlie gave her life to protect the world from.

The world is ignorant to this. Unaware of the sacrifice that Charlie made. And that was her choice. A choice that consigned the Bad Man and his evil to obscurity and shut him away for ever.

About the Author

Jed Cope is the author of seven Ben and Thom books. He has also penned five further books and a collection of short stories. He is working industriously to add to that number in the mistaken belief that he will be given a day off from writing once he's written his twentieth novel. Unfortunately, his captors got distracted by an ice cream van that had been converted into a travelling pub and completely forgot about Jed. Still, I'm sure it'll all turn out fine in the end. Usually does in circumstances such as these.

This isn't Jed's first foray into the horror genre. Not only has he read almost everything that Stephen King has written, including the graffiti on *that* toilet wall, but he also lives in a dark and twisted world where the truth of it is always worse than the fiction we create in order to get by and survive.

There will be more horror, of that you can be sure.

As well as gullible and well-meaning, Jed is a charismatic, enigmatic and pneumatic sort. Having retired from a successful career as a secret multiple F1 Champion, octopus whisperer and technology trillionaire, Jed was abducted from his underground shed where he was working on the next generation of psychic begonias, to do what he does best; make things up.

You can connect with me on:
- https://twitter.com/jed_cope
- https://www.facebook.com/jedcopeauthor

Also by Jed Cope

So far, there are seven Ben and Thom Books:
  The Chair Who Loved Me
  Are Bunnies Electric?
  Smell My Cheese!
  Death and Taxis
  Oh Ben and Thom, Where Art Thou?
  Something Merkin This Way Comes
  Mrs Ben's Boys

Book Eight is a twinkle in the author's eye, but that twinkle is a determined wee beggar and it has a habit of making its way out into the world, so watch this space!

There's a children's Ben and Thom Book:
  If Only... The Adventures of an Intergalactic Chair

And five further books that have nothing whatsoever to do with Ben and Thom:
  The Pipe
  The Entrepreneur's Club
  Two for the Show
  Fly Me to the Moon
  The Rules of Life

And a collection of short stories:
  Locked, Down and Short

Jed intends to add to the list before you've finished reading this one. It's what he does.

Printed in Great Britain
by Amazon